"What in the world?"

Don's mutter drew Caroline's attention. His gaze was fixed on a truck bearing down on them at a rapid speed from the opposite direction. Don slowed and edged as close to the side of the roadway as possible. The truck mirrored their movement without slowing.

Gripping the door handle, Caroline tried to breathe past the knot of apprehension tightening her chest. The older model Ford truck seemed intent on playing some sort of game of chicken as it roared ever closer, directly in their path.

"Don?"

"Hang on!"

At the last second Don revved the motor and swerved to the other side of the road, out of the path of the oncoming vehicle.

Caroline twisted in her seat to stare after the truck until it roared out of sight.

"That was random, right?" She worked to calm her heart rate.

"Given someone stalked you, broke into your apartment, then bombed said apartment? No."

Books by Terri Reed

TERRI REED

At an early age Terri Reed discovered the wonderful world of fiction and declared she would one day write a book. Now she is fulfilling that dream and enjoys writing for Love Inspired Books. Her second book, *A Sheltering Love,* was a 2006 RITA® Award finalist and a 2005 National Readers' Choice Award finalist. Her book *Strictly Confidential,* book five of the Faith at the Crossroads continuity series, took third place in the 2007 American Christian Fiction Writers Book of the Year Award, and *Her Christmas Protector* took third place in 2008. She is an active member of both Romance Writers of America and American Christian Fiction Writers. She resides in the Pacific Northwest with her college-sweetheart husband, two wonderful children and an array of critters. When not writing, she enjoys spending time with her family and friends, gardening and playing with her dogs.

You can write to Terri at P.O. Box 19555, Portland, OR 97280. Visit her on the web at www.loveinspiredauthors.com, leave comments on her blog at www.ladiesofsuspense.blogspot.com or email her at terrireed@sterling.net.

THE SECRET
HEIRESS

Terri Reed

Love Inspired

Recycling programs
for this product may
not exist in your area.

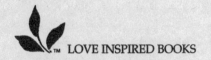 LOVE INSPIRED BOOKS

ISBN-13: 978-0-373-44472-4

THE SECRET HEIRESS

Copyright © 2012 by Terri Reed

This edition published by arrangement with Love Inspired Books.

® and TM are trademarks of Love Inspired Books, used under license.
Trademarks indicated with ® are registered in the United States Patent
and Trademark Office, the Canadian Trade Marks Office and in other
countries.

www.LoveInspiredBooks.com

Printed in U.S.A.

Dear Reader,

Welcome to Love Inspired!

2012 is a very special year for us. It marks the fifteenth anniversary of Love Inspired Books. Hard to believe that fifteen years ago, we first began publishing our warm and wonderful inspirational romances.

Back in 1997, we offered readers three books a month. Since then we've expanded quite a bit! In addition to the heartwarming contemporary romances of Love Inspired, we have the exciting romantic suspenses of Love Inspired Suspense, and the adventurous historical romances of Love Inspired Historical. Whatever your reading preference, we've got fourteen books a month for you to choose from now!

Throughout the year we'll be celebrating in several different ways. Look for books by bestselling authors who've been writing for us since the beginning, stories by brand-new authors you won't want to miss, special miniseries in all three lines, reissues of top authors, and much, much more.

This is our way of thanking you for reading Love Inspired books. We know our uplifting stories of hope, faith and love touch your hearts as much as they touch ours.

Join us in celebrating fifteen amazing years of inspirational romance!

Blessings,

Melissa Endlich and Tina James

Senior Editors of Love Inspired Books

I'd like to say a special thank you to my editors at Love Inspired for your expertise and guidance in making my books the best they can be.

Thank you also to Melissa, Lissa, Leah and Ruth for your support and encouragement.

* * *

For you did not receive the spirit of bondage again to fear, but you received the Spirit of adoption by who we cry out, "Abba, Father." The Spirit Himself bears witness with our spirit that we are children of God, and if children, then heirs—heirs of God and joint heirs with Christ, if indeed we suffer with Him, that we may also be glorified together.
—*Romans* 8:15–17

ONE

"Hey, Cavanaugh, lady here to see you."

Amid the buzz of conversations, phones ringing and the faint sound of keyboards that served as background noise at the offices of Trent Associates, Donovan Cavanaugh saved the document he was working on—the final report on the case he'd just wrapped up.

A real doozy. He'd provided protection for a manager turned whistleblower of a pharmaceutical company. The guy's conscience hadn't allowed him to ignore the release of a drug with adverse side effects, regardless of the company bigwigs wanting to make all the money they could without informing the public of the hazards.

He pushed his chair away from the desk. "Name?"

"Gorgeous. At least that's what I'd name her," Kyle Martin said from the doorway of the "war room," the place where each Trent employee had his or her own space—desk, phone, laptop and file cabinet—within the brownstone of Boston's Back Bay neighborhood that housed the protection specialists agency. Kyle grinned, his too-handsome face beaming, making him look younger than twenty-nine.

Okay, the laid-back attitude helped make the perennial surfer dude seem young, too. But Don knew better than to underestimate his colleague, no matter how young he looked. Kyle was good at what he did. He'd been a SEAL before James Trent brought him on board. Those guys were as tough as they were smart.

Dubbed the best in the business of protection, Trent Associates employed ten operatives, all highly trained with either a background in military like Don or in law enforcement.

"Did Gorgeous say what she wanted?"

Kyle wiggled his eyebrows. "You, dude. She wants *you*."

A low whistle came from Don's right. Ex-paratrooper and definite ladies' man Trevor Jordan smirked. "Sounds interesting. Something we should know about?"

Ignoring Trevor's and the other curious glances aimed his way, Don strode to the door. "Where's Lisa?" The young woman who usually manned the agency's front desk would have been more discreet in announcing a potential client.

"On lunch break." Kyle dogged his steps down the hall. "I'm covering the front desk."

A smart retort froze on Don's tongue the second his gaze landed on the petite brunette dwarfed by the ten-foot-tall Christmas tree in the "client" room just off the entryway. She had her back to him, but he didn't need to see her face to recognize the pretty woman who'd once captured his attention.

She inspected an ornament. A gold, sparkly star. Her small, delicate hands trembled.

As the name "Gorgeous" echoed with unerring accuracy inside his head, he forced out her real name. "Caroline?"

She turned around. Her big amber-colored eyes were wide, the pupils dilated. A square white bandage, in stark contrast to her olive skin, covered half her forehead. Not that anything could mar her looks. She was still as beautiful as he remembered.

He hated the vulnerability he saw on her pretty face. Concern and something distinctly protective hammered at him. "What's going on?"

Tears shimmered in her eyes. "Don, I need to hire you. Someone's trying to kill me."

Absorbing the announcement with surprise, Don was at her side in two strides.

"Come, sit down." He took her by the arm and led her to one of the cushy sofas. "Tell me what's happened so we can figure out what to do next."

"I—" She took a shuddering breath. "When I got home from work yesterday, my apartment door had been wired with explosives. The police are investigating."

Don sucked in a sharp breath of shock. A bomb. His right hand flexed, stretching the scar tissue along the outer edge. His gaze went to the bandage on her head. "Are you okay?"

She touched her fingertip to her forehead. "Yes. A mild concussion. My hearing still isn't completely back, since part of my front door hit me in the head."

He sent up a silent prayer of thanksgiving that she hadn't suffered worse injury. There was no mistaking the fear on her face. He understood. He'd felt the same way the first time he'd faced a life-threatening situation during his military tour. Only time and repeated exposure to danger had dulled the panic. His faith had kept him sane. But this wasn't a war zone. Caroline shouldn't have to be afraid in her own home.

"You did the right thing coming here. Start from the beginning. Tell me everything."

Visibly shaking, she nodded.

He gathered her cold hands in his and rubbed them. Appreciation flared in her eyes.

"For a month, I kept seeing the same man hanging around my apartment building, my shop, even the grocery store. Then last week my apartment was broken into. The intruder left the place a mess and yet nothing was missing, as far as I could tell. The police thought maybe I'd interrupted the thieves before they could take anything. Then two days ago I received this letter from a lawyer in Mississippi." She removed an envelope from her purse and handed it to him. "At first I thought it was a hoax or scam or something."

He opened the letter and read the contents.

Dear Ms. Tully,
I'm writing on behalf of the Maddox Estate, of which you may be named coheir as we have reason to believe you are Isabella Maddox's daughter. There are conditions, however, that must be met. Please contact me at your earliest convenience to discuss the next steps.

"You'd never heard of this lawyer, Randall Paladin?"

"No, I hadn't."

He wasn't sure what to make of the letter. "So you contacted him?"

"First, I did some research. I didn't want to call just

to get pulled into some kind of scam. But the Maddox family is certainly real. They've lived in Mississippi for the past two centuries. And Mr. Paladin is an established lawyer in the same community."

She took a breath. "You see, I was adopted as a baby. A closed adoption."

He hadn't known that. But then again, they hadn't really known each other well. He'd made sure of that.

"So I called Mr. Paladin. Elijah Maddox recently discovered that his daughter, Isabella, had given up a child twenty-seven years ago. He had no idea who the father could be."

"And he's sure Isabella's baby is you?"

She nodded. "So he claims. I asked about DNA testing to be sure, but Mr. Paladin said they have conclusive evidence already."

"The not-so-random break-in. They were after your DNA."

"Mr. Maddox hired a private investigator to find me. I guess he wanted to be sure of who I was before he reported back." Her anxious expression tore at him. "But what's more troubling is the other thing I found in my research—Isabella Maddox was murdered."

His gut clenched. "Was her killer brought to justice?"

Her mouth twisted in an aggravated frown. "I don't have any details. The newspaper articles I found didn't mention any trial, and Mr. Paladin wouldn't give me any further information about her when I tried to ask. He only wanted to talk about the new will Mr. Maddox had drawn up. He said in order for me to secure a place in Elijah Maddox's estate I must go to Mississippi and stay with the Maddox family from Christmas Eve through New Year's."

"They can't legally compel you to do this." Wariness took hold. "Why would they want you to come there? And why specifically those dates?"

"He wouldn't say, only that it was important that I do."

Ridiculous. "You're not thinking of going."

A determined light entered her tawny-colored gaze. "I have to." Her expression implored him to understand. "Not for the money, though. I've been looking for my birth parents since I was eighteen. I need to know who these people are and what happened to my birth mother. Besides, I wouldn't be any safer staying here. My apartment door is proof enough of that." She touched his scarred hand. "Will you take me on as a client and accompany me?"

As she waited for an answer, he hesitated as a firestorm of sensation raced up his arm. He cleared his throat. "Trent Associates can help you."

Relief swept across her face. "I knew I made the right decision contacting you after all you did to keep Kristina safe."

He'd been protecting socialite Kristina Worthington when he'd met Caroline in the course of his assignment. The two women were good friends. "Nice of you to think of me."

The corners of her mouth lifted in a small smile. Her gaze caressed his face, filling him with a fierce compulsion to gather her into his arms.

Uh-oh. He was pulling a Carlucci. He inhaled sharply, reining in his attraction. Not going to happen. Don was a professional. He played by the rules. Because doing so was the only way to guarantee any amount of success.

A few months back Trent had hired ex-Secret Service agent Anthony Carlucci. But during his first assignment—protecting the widow of a murdered U.S. senator—the guy up and fell in love with his protectee. As soon as she was safe, he'd proposed, and decided to go to work for the Department of Justice. Don's boss, James Trent, had declared this a good thing for Trent Associates. Now they had a trusted contact in the D.O.J. to call on when needed.

Maybe.

But in Don's book, Carlucci had crossed the line. He should have bowed out of the assignment the second he realized his feelings had turned personal. That would have been the right thing, the honorable thing, to do.

The second most important Rule of Protection— don't get emotionally involved with clients. Doing so impaired judgment and put everyone involved in danger.

If he was already so easily distracted by Caroline then it was time for reinforcements.

"Stay here." He rose from the sofa. "I'll be right back."

Don hustled upstairs and knocked on his boss's door.

"Enter," came James Trent's muffled invitation.

Don stepped inside the large office. Natural light from the high, arched windows gleamed on the mahogany floor. James sat at his massive desk. Wiry and full of energy, he smiled and waved Don closer.

Rather than sit in the chair facing the desk, Don paced and quickly detailed Caroline's predicament.

James steepled his hands, his elbows resting on the

desk, making Don feel like an errant teen facing the principal.

"So what is your plan?"

Don cleared his throat and hardened his resolve. "Actually, sir, I was thinking it would be better if Simone or Jackie were assigned to Ms. Tully."

Simone Walker was an ex-homicide detective for the Detroit Police Department, while Jackie Blain had been a deputy sheriff for some small Midwest town before moving to Boston and joining Trent Associates.

A crease appeared between James's eyebrows. "Really? Why is that?"

Don hooked a finger in the collar of his gray sweater, needing a bit of the cold December air. "Their law-enforcement backgrounds would be useful in this situation."

"If Ms. Tully wants a full-scale investigation she needs to go to the police or hire a private investigator," James said.

"She's already been to the police. What she wants now is protection on her trip to Mississippi."

"Then you sound perfect for the job."

The only way to arrange the best protection for Caroline was to be straightforward with James. "I have a prior history with Ms. Tully."

"Oh?" James's gaze narrowed, belying the laugh lines at the corners of his eyes. "Do tell."

"I met Ms. Tully last year while on assignment guarding Kristina Worthington. The two are close friends."

"And?"

"There was…attraction." She'd been the first woman in a long time to capture Don's notice and make him yearn for something he wasn't sure he'd ever be able to have—a committed relationship.

"How long did you date?"

Don dropped his chin and stared at his boss. "She was part of an assignment, sir. We didn't date."

Though she'd given off signals suggesting she'd have been receptive to his attention.

"Ah." A gleam entered James eyes. "Did she ask for you specifically today, or did you draw the short straw?"

Don swallowed, sensing a trap. "She asked for me, sir."

Like a Cheshire cat, James smiled. "Then you'll have to figure out how to put your personal attraction and feelings aside, because she obviously trusts you enough to ask for your help."

"But, sir, she needs twenty-four-hour protection. I'm not a good fit for that." Even as the words left his mouth he knew James would see through the bogus excuse. He'd provided around-the-clock security for numerous women and children. Just none who had made his heart pound or his blood race.

A droll look crossed James's face. "Didn't you say this woman is a friend of the Worthingtons? They're very good clients."

James stood and rounded the desk, halting to put a hand on Don's shoulder. "You'll do fine. You're a professional. Though I must say it's entertaining to finally see you a little flustered."

Don opened his mouth to protest, but James was already walking toward the door.

"I'd like to meet Ms. Tully and assure her you'll be taking her case," James said before exiting.

Don sat for a moment, trying to come to terms with what had just happened. He'd come to James's office intending to have someone else assigned to Caroline. For both their sakes.

Too bad his plan backfired. Big time.

Caroline glanced toward the staircase Don had quickly ascended. Would he take her on as a client?

Seeking help from Don had seemed like such a good idea when she was in the hospital yesterday, but now... The instant she'd seen him, she'd been flooded with overwhelming relief and something else—something close to a coming-home feeling that both astounded and confused her. She barely knew him, yet it had taken all her strength not to sink to the floor in a heap of relief beneath that big beautiful Christmas tree as soon as he came near. It was almost like a part of her knew she could relax, that she was safe with him. How strange to feel such trust for a man, especially one she barely knew. But now that he'd walked away, fear was returning.

She clasped her hands tightly together to still the evidence of the tremors racing along her limbs.

For so many years, she'd hoped and prayed that she'd someday find her family. But now her dream was turning into a nightmare. Who wanted her dead, and why? Was she truly in danger from her newfound family? How could she possibly face it without Don by her side?

Don appeared pretty much as she remembered. The same honey-blond hair cut short around his ears and collar and a little longer on top. Same tall, muscular frame that made him look like he could carry the weight of the world and not be bothered by the load.

The dove-gray sweater he wore so well emphasized his broad shoulders.

His eyes drew her in as before, too. Inviting liquid pools of teal reflecting the firelight from the hearth.

She wanted to melt into his gaze and forget the past few days. Not a good idea. She wasn't looking for a romance, had no intention of putting her heart at risk again. Even with Don, a man whom she hadn't been able to forget this past year. She only needed Don to protect her.

Acutely aware of the throbbing in her temples and the ache in her back from the blast slamming her into the wall the previous day, she shifted gingerly against the sofa's rich chintz fabric covering and focused on her surroundings rather than her pain. Crown molding, high-quality furniture and an understated color scheme in muted rose and greens created a pleasing atmosphere in the waiting room. The Christmas tree added a nice, homey touch and the fresh scent of pine. She liked the warm and comfortable feel of Trent Associates. She hadn't really been sure what to expect, since she'd never been here.

Or hired a bodyguard. She could barely believe she was hiring one now. But she knew it wouldn't be safe to go to Mississippi alone. Honestly, it probably wasn't safe to go to Mississippi at all—but she wasn't going to let that stop her.

She'd been truthful when she'd told Don she didn't want Mr. Maddox's money. At least not for herself— her dress boutique had a booming business despite the troubled economy. There were charities she supported that could use the funds.

But learning more about her birth mother and the

family whose DNA she shared was important to her. She had so many unanswered questions.

It wasn't that she didn't love her parents—the older couple who'd adopted and raised her. She loved them with every fiber of her being.

But a part of her had always felt out of place. Her dark hair and olive complexion made it obvious she didn't belong in a statuesque family of Swedish descent. She was the odd duck, the outsider. Though she never questioned her adoptive parents' love for her, she'd always longed for a more basic sense of connection.

The front door opened and two women walked in, distracting Caroline from her thoughts. The tall brunette, her hair slicked back into a French twist, wore a sleek black coat and knee-high black, low-heeled boots. The very picture of sophistication. In contrast, the other woman had a wild head of blond curls and a very animated face. Plus, she was tiny. Even more petite than Caroline. Her clunky bright pink snow boots made squishy noises on the hardwood floor as the two women walked past and disappeared down the hall.

More bodyguards? Okay, the dark one looked the part, maybe. But the other? She looked more like a kindergarten teacher.

Footsteps sounded on the stairs. Caroline lifted her gaze, hoping for Don's return, but instead a well-dressed man, closer to fifty, approached. Though not nearly as tall as Don, there was nothing diminutive about him. His craggy face showed a life well lived. A quiet strength inspiring trust emanated from him as he sat beside Caroline on the sofa. He stuck out his hand. "Ms. Tully, I'm James Trent."

Bemused and impressed that the man behind the

name of the company was seeing her personally, she slipped her hand into his. "Mr. Trent."

He covered her hand in a fatherly gesture. She suddenly longed for her parents, the people who loved her. She didn't go home to New Hampshire nearly often enough. She vowed to make a better effort to spend time with her mother and father.

"Don explained your situation," James said. "I have every confidence in his ability to keep you safe."

The tension inside of Caroline eased. Don would be her bodyguard. She'd be safe in his care. She felt almost light-headed with gratitude.

Don stepped into the room. His features that moments ago had shown compassion and kindness were now as hard as granite. His square jaw looked firm, his blue-green eyes watchful, but guarded.

She tilted her head, unsure why he'd become so cool.

Then she noticed he'd put on a shoulder holster. It held a big, black gun against his left side. A shiver tripped over her.

"I'll escort you to Mississippi, Ms. Tully," Don said.

Ms. Tully? Was he kidding? Her gaze darted to Mr. Trent. Was Don acting so weird and formal because of his boss? "Thank you, Mr. Cavanaugh. Mr. Trent."

Trent patted her hand before rising from the sofa. "Don't worry, Ms. Tully. You'll be well protected."

"I know," she murmured, her gaze on Don.

Don inclined his head in deference to his boss as the man left the room. Then he turned to her, his expression still hard and unreadable. Mr. Trent was gone, so why was Don still being so distant?

"Where are you staying?" he asked.

"With the Burkes," she replied. Kristina and her

homicide-detective husband, Gabe, had been adamant she stay in their guest bedroom until the investigation was over. She'd gratefully accepted.

"We have a lot to arrange before we head south."

She grasped his outstretched hand. Their palms pressed together. Her fingers curled automatically around his as he pulled her to her feet. She didn't want to let go. His touch not only warmed, but made her feel connected to him. And kicked up an anxious flutter inside for yearning for that connection.

Not going there, she reminded herself. Ever. Again.

She extracted her hand. "How do we explain your presence in Mississippi?"

His mouth twisted in a grim smile. "I'm your new fiancé."

Two days later, Caroline sat next to Don on a plane bound for Jackson, Mississippi. Though the police were still investigating the bombing of her apartment, they had yet to find a suspect. The lead detective had said he'd contact her if they came up with any answers. He saw no reason she should stick close. He did warn her to be careful. That was what Don was for. To make sure she was cared for. Safe.

Anticipation bubbled in her tummy.

Once she'd made the decision to journey south to the Maddox estate, everything had come together in a whirl of activity. She'd called Mr. Paladin to explain that she and her fiancé would be coming. He'd made the necessary preparations for their arrival.

After arranging for her assistant to take care of Caroline's clothing store through the holidays, she and Don traveled to New Hampshire to explain to her parents why she wouldn't be spending Christmas with them.

Telling them had been hard, but they'd understood her need to know where she came from. Love for the people who'd raised her filled her heart to overflowing. She thanked God for giving her Evangeline and Herbert Tully. They made plans to celebrate Christmas together after her return. Wanting to keep them from worrying, she refrained from telling them about the attempt on her life. And while she explained that her mother was deceased, she didn't admit that Isabella had been murdered.

"You okay?"

She slanted a glance at Don. "Nervous."

"Understandable."

Don had researched the Maddox family beyond what she had been able to find. Apparently, Trent Associates had enough law enforcement connections to do some real digging. Caroline had been fascinated by what he'd told her of the family's history...but she'd been very disturbed by what he'd learned about her mother's death in New Orleans twenty-seven years ago. The case had never been solved. A ripple of unease cascaded over her at the thought of it.

Even if Caroline found answers to some of her questions, other questions would remain unanswered—like who killed her mother and why?

Don's warm hand covered hers, comfort sweeping up her arm and chasing away her distress. She turned her hand and held on, needing his strength.

Not good. Not good at all. He was her pretend fiancé. They didn't have to pretend when it was only the two of them alone. But she couldn't bring herself to withdraw her hand.

Thirty minutes after touchdown they were on their way in a compact rental with a map of the area. The rental car agent had drawn out the quickest route from Jackson to the Maddox estate in Jefferson County in the middle of the Mississippi Valley.

Low, gray clouds had hovered menacingly when they started driving. Half an hour later, they opened up to a torrent of rain. The rhythmic swoosh of the wipers and the hum of the tires on the road were the only sounds as Don drove.

The rural landscape was vastly different from her beloved New England. Flat, green fields extended for acres on both sides of the highway, dotted by the occasional modest home, rusted car or abandoned farm equipment overgrown with weeds. It all looked so lonely and desolate.

Caroline consulted the map, then pointed to a sign that read Fayette Road. "It looks like we turn right up here."

They left the main highway for a more rural road. Another turn put them on a narrow, unpaved road that ran along a creek. Tall pine and hardwoods provided some relief from the pelting rain but there was no respite from the hot, choking humidity, even with the air conditioning on. Her winter wool jacket wasn't very practical for this climate. She hadn't thought to check the weather or even bring an umbrella. Her mind had been focused on meeting her biological family and learning something—anything—about the woman who'd given birth to her.

"What in the world?"

Don's mutter drew Caroline's attention. His gaze was fixed on a truck bearing down on them at a rapid speed from the opposite direction. Don slowed and edged as close to the side of the roadway as possible. Trees and brush lined the road, their branches scratching the paint of the car. The truck mirrored their movement without slowing.

Gripping the door handle, Caroline tried to breathe past the knot of apprehension tightening her chest. The older model Ford truck seemed intent on playing some sort of game of chicken as it roared ever closer, directly in their path.

"Don?"

"Hang on!"

At the last second Don revved the motor and swerved to the other side of the road out of the path of the oncoming vehicle. The truck passed close to the passenger side in a rain-splashed whirl of color. Caroline couldn't make out the driver's face, only that he wore a baseball cap.

Don accelerated. Caroline twisted in her seat to stare after the truck until it roared out of sight.

"That was random, right?" She worked to calm her heart rate.

"Given someone stalked you, broke into your apartment, then bombed said apartment? No."

Dread chilled her blood. "This incident can't be related to… I mean, how would anyone know what kind of vehicle we rented and that we'd be on this road at this time?"

"I don't know. But apparently someone is keeping tabs on your movements." He slanted her a glance as the car slowed to a normal speed. "We could turn back and go home right now."

She shook her head. "No. Whoever is after me clearly knows where to find me. Running won't help. And it won't give me any answers about my family."

He gave a rueful shake of his head and resumed staring out the front window. Tension rolled off him in waves, making her taut nerves stretch tighter.

"The road leading to the Maddox estate shouldn't be much farther," she said.

At the five-mile mark, Don turned the car down a long graveled drive. Large trees lined the road, their spindly branches tangling together overhead to form a canopy. Soon the tree line ended, opening up to a flat lawn stretching on either side eventually leading to more trees.

A large, two-story, redbrick home with a white colonnade across the front came into view at the end of the drive.

Through the pouring rain, Caroline studied the structure.

At first glance it appeared majestic, as if they'd stumbled on an old pre-Civil War movie set. But soon she started noticing signs of decay and disrepair. They passed a shed that looked ready to crumble and a more modern detached garage big enough for at least three cars. It seemed more stable than the shed—but not by much. As they drew closer to the main house, she noticed the peeling paint on the columns, the brown and green moss creeping up the edges of the foundation. Several of the cracked blue window shutters hung off their hinges.

The old plantation home appeared uncared for, resembling something more fitting for a horrible B slasher movie than a wealthy Southern family at Christmas time. No festive decorations spruced up the place. No sign of celebration at all. A stark contrast to her parents' home with twinkling lights, a glittering tree visible through the front bay window, and a nativity scene on the front lawn.

A shiver of disquiet skated across her flesh. Maybe she really had made a mistake in coming here. This felt all wrong—nothing at all as she'd imagined when she thought of coming here. Maybe she should have left well enough alone.

No. She squared her shoulders, determined not to back down now.

Don parked at the foot of a set of crooked stairs leading to the front entrance. "This isn't exactly the prosperous Southern estate I expected."

More misgivings stirred. "I don't get it. Someone tried to kill me for this?"

"Looks can be deceiving."

"True."

"Not too late to turn back."

Keeping her gaze on the house, she shook her head. Now was not the time to lose her courage.

"Okay, then." He shrugged into his water-resistant coat. "You ready?"

Not really. Her pulse pounded in her ears. Nervous tingles made her feel a bit queasy. Pushing her anxiety aside, she quickly buttoned her jacket to protect her blouse from the steady stream of rain.

Forcing herself to appear more confident than she felt, she nodded. "Yes. I need to do this."

They exited the car and hustled up the stairs to the

porch under the overhang. Humidity hung in the air, making her rethink the buttoning of her coat. Empty wooden rockers creaked in the blowing wind. The faint noise of dogs barking unchecked somewhere in the distance accentuated how different this country setting was from her life in Boston, where animal control would be called for such a racket.

She shook out her loose hair. Water dripped down the collar of her coat, the sensation causing a chill despite the mild temperature. She must have shuddered because Don stepped closer, his protection as enveloping and unspoken as the warmth radiating off him.

The wide, wooden front door swung open with a creak that gave her the same creepy feeling as if she were watching a horror movie and the unsuspecting hero and heroine were about to find themselves in peril. What utter nonsense! She gave herself a mental shake.

A tall, lean man stood on the threshold. He wore a sorely outdated dark suit and a white dress shirt that needed some bleach. His gray eyes studied Caroline as if she were a piece of artwork and he sought the flaw.

She smiled, though she felt more like squirming. "Hello. I'm Caroline Tully. You should be expecting me."

Solemnly, the man nodded and stepped back. "Come in. I'm Horace," the man said in a nasal drawl. His gaze flicked to the sky. "Nasty weather we're having. The weatherman says the rain will continue on 'til New Year's."

Not sure what to do with that tidbit of information, Caroline stepped inside. Don kept his hand at her back, the pressure soothing.

"I'll tell Mr. Maddox you've arrived," Horace said

with a deferential nod before quietly disappearing down the hall.

"Interesting place," Don muttered.

Caroline nodded in agreement. "Most of the furniture looks like it's been here since the house was built."

Despite the graceful and refined lines of the Federal style furnishings, the pieces did little to impress or offer welcome. The rose-colored damask material covering the horseshoe-shaped seats on two fiddleback chairs had faded to a lackluster hue. Everything looked worn and threadbare, including a thick and tattered leather-bound Bible that sat on an oil varnished table. The gold lettering on the cover was nearly worn away.

A hutch loaded with dusty books sat against the wall beside an arched doorway. She noticed there were no signs of Christmas here, either, regardless of the presence of a Bible.

Not even a hint of the commercialism of the season, no mistletoe in the arched doorways, no tree, snowmen or Santas, even.

No nativity set commemorating the true meaning of the holiday.

The strange sensation of being watched raised the fine hairs at the nape of Caroline's neck. She tensed and searched for the source.

Scarred hardwood floors stretched across the entryway and fed into a wide staircase with an ornately carved banister leading to the second story where two teens, a boy and a girl, waited at the top. Both had raven hair and light hazel eyes.

Caroline smiled a greeting. Neither teen smiled back.

Creeped-out, she glanced at Don. He'd been watching the teenagers, too. He met her gaze and shrugged.

The butler returned. The teenagers scurried out of sight. "Mr. Maddox will see you now."

A flutter of nerves hit Caroline as they followed Horace up the stairs and down the hall to the other end of the second story. He opened a door and stepped aside.

The room was shrouded in shadows. The curtains were closed and only a small table lamp in the corner glowed near a full-size bed where a wizened old man lay. Thinning silver hair covered his head. He stared at her with bloodshot eyes and lifted a hand, beckoning them closer. "Isabella?"

Heart hammering in her chest, Caroline walked forward. She wasn't sure what to say to this obviously ill man. Her grandfather. Compassion filled her, as it would for anyone brought low by sickness. She took his hand in hers. His skin had darkened on his arm and felt clammy, and the bones were so fragile. "No, I'm Caroline. And this is…my fiancé, Don."

The old man seemed to shrink a little. "I'm sorry," Elijah Maddox said in a raspy voice. "I shouldn't have brought you here, child. It's not safe."

Stunned, Caroline glanced at Don. Good thing she had him to protect her.

A thundercloud of anger darkened Don's expression. He stepped closer. "So you know someone has tried to kill her?"

Elijah's eyes widened. "No!" He closed his eyes for a moment, a spasm of pain crossed his bony features. When he opened his eyes, real fear shone bright in the amber depths. He looked toward the door then back to Caroline. "Someone's killing me!"

TWO

Don's blood pressure skyrocketed. His fists clenched. He'd known coming here was a bad idea. "Why would you summon Caroline if you knew she'd be in danger?"

"I didn't know. Not when I sent Willard to find her," Elijah insisted.

"Who's Willard?" Don asked.

"A local private investigator." His rheumy gaze pleaded for understanding. "I thought I was dying so I sent for you. But by the time I realized that someone wanted me dead, it was too late—you were already on your way."

Distress played over Caroline's face. "Why do you think someone is trying to kill you?"

Elijah shook his head. "Not trying. Succeeding. The doctor says I should be getting better but I'm not."

"What sickness do you have?" Don asked.

"Addison's disease. Or so the doctor claims." His bushy gray eyebrows drew together. "No one believes me that there's more to it than that."

Don exchanged a dubious glance with Caroline.

"What is Addison's?" Caroline asked.

"My adrenal glands aren't producing enough of their

hormones, allowing my immune system to attack the glands. But Addison's can be controlled with medication. I should be getting better, and instead…" He gestured around him.

"Have you sought a second opinion?" she asked.

"Dr. Reese is the only doctor around. I've asked to have a doctor from Jackson come in. Samuel said he'd see to it after the holidays. I might not make it that long."

"Why not go to the nearest hospital?" Don asked.

Elijah frowned with frustration. "I don't like hospitals. The doctor can come to me. But no one will call him."

"Why do you think someone wants you dead?" Don pressed, unsure what to believe, but needing answers so he could keep Caroline safe.

The old man snorted beneath his breath. "Greed, why else? Once I'm gone—" He paused as a spasm of pain twisted his wrinkled face.

Don's thoughts turned to Samuel Maddox. Caroline's uncle, Isabella's brother. Don might not have a background in investigative work, but he knew the first rule—follow the money. Was Samuel the one behind the attempt on Caroline's life and his father's? He had the most to gain and the most to lose. "You named Caroline as a coheir in your will. I assume your son, Samuel, is the other heir."

"Yes. I've made provisions for his family of course, and the staff. But Samuel and Isabella's child are my heirs."

He searched Caroline's face. "You look so much like Isabella. When you walked in, I thought I was seeing her again."

Caroline blinked. "I do?"

The wistful note in her tone brought an ache to Don's chest.

"Where is she buried?" Caroline asked.

Elijah dropped his gaze. Anguish washed over his face. "Fayette Cemetery. In the family plot next to her mother."

"Can you tell us what happened to her?" Don asked. Though he'd read the brief report the NOPD sent to Trent, he wanted to learn what the family knew.

Torment filled the old man's face. "Murdered. My baby was murdered."

Blunt force trauma to the back of the head. The weapon used had been the base of a brass table lamp. The police found no fingerprints in the apartment other than Isabella's suggesting the killer had worn gloves.

The heartbreak on Caroline's face twisted Don's insides into knots. A fat tear rolled slowly down her cheek, leaving a wet trail. Don fought the urge to pull her close and soothe away her tears. A real fiancé would. But he wasn't her fiancé. Not even close.

A clap of thunder exploded in the charged silence. Don flinched, the sound triggering old terrors, old memories. Caroline reached for his hand and held on tight. The warmth of her touch grounded him in the moment and made him feel needed as a man, not just as a bodyguard.

Oh, brother, he was treading in deep water here.

"The police said it was a burglary gone bad," Elijah said. His brow furrowed. "Except..."

"Except?" Don probed. The police report stated there were jewelry and other items missing, leading them to suspect robbery as the motive.

"The lead detective told me there was no forced entry."

A cold knot of apprehension fisted in Don's gut. Isabella Maddox had opened the door to her killer. A far different situation than a random intruder. That wasn't in the report he'd read. Something wasn't right about Isabella Maddox's murder. But he wasn't an investigator nor was it his job to solve a cold case. His sole intent was to protect Caroline.

"Does that mean she knew her attacker?" Shock reverberated in Caroline's voice.

"Maybe. It could have been someone delivering something or a repair man. But whichever the case, it wasn't random." She'd been targeted. Like Caroline. But was Isabella's death related to the threat against Caroline? This situation kept getting more complicated every minute.

"When was she…killed?" Caroline's voice was barely above a whisper.

"October 20, twenty-seven years ago."

Caroline made a strangled sound. "I was born September 30."

She leaned into Don as if her legs suddenly couldn't support her. The need to protect rose sharply. Only this wasn't a physical threat, but an emotional one. Don was out of his comfort zone. The best he could do was to remove her from the situation, allow her time to come to terms with the information she'd learned of her birth mother's death and try to talk her into leaving—hiding somewhere until the police found the person who had tried to kill her. He let go of her hand, took her by the shoulders and steered her toward the door.

She went willingly but as they reached the threshold she stopped abruptly. "He's in danger."

"It could be the ravings of a dying man," Don insisted in a low voice.

Caroline wiped at her tears. "We have to find out for sure."

"No, we should leave now before the storm gets any worse."

Proud and beautiful, she held his gaze, her chin at a defiant angle, her shoulders squared. "Gorgeous" wouldn't be swayed. "I'm not leaving until I know what's going on. If someone is hurting him then it's up to us to stop it."

Determined. Stubborn. And courageous. A potent mix that could get her killed. Respect for this gutsy lady grew even as he prepared to counter any argument. "If a crime is being committed, it's up to the *police* to stop it. You're not any safer here than he is. Remember, someone tried to kill you. That person could be in this house."

"Of course I'm safe. I have you."

Her confidence in his abilities sent pleasure curling through his system. He hoped he lived up to her expectations.

Her gaze shifted back toward her grandfather. "He needs protection. If what he claims is true, then he must be a victim of the same person who has been attacking me." The plea in her eyes tugged at Don. "Please, we have to help him."

Don lifted a hand to capture one last stray tear that fell from her lovely amber eyes. "You have such a tender and stubborn heart."

A smile touched her lips and pleasure lit up her eyes. "Does that mean we'll stay? You'll protect both of us?"

Did he have a choice? Yes. But he couldn't walk away and leave her here alone. He had a job to do. He'd see it through to the end. "We can talk to his doctor and find out what's going on with his health."

"That's a start." She walked back toward her grandfather. "How do we contact Dr. Reese?"

"Ask Horace or Mary," Elijah said, his raspy voice sounding weak.

Don started forward. "Mary?"

"Mary is Horace's wife."

A sharp burst of thunder rattled the window. On its heels followed a loud explosion that shuddered through the house. The sound filled the room, close and intense. What little light the lamp provided winked out throwing the room into blackness. Caroline let out a startled squawk echoed by another female shriek farther away in the house. Somewhere outside, dogs barked.

Acting on training and instinct, Don pulled Caroline to the floor and covered her with his body. For a split second, he was catapulted back in time to Afghanistan. His unit had been pinned down under enemy fire in Kandahar. Screams of dying soldiers surrounded him. The dust of mortar shells demolishing the walls of the building where they'd taken refuge filled his nostrils. He could still feel the grit on his skin, in his eyes. Feel the despair building in his chest. The unspoken prayer on his tongue…

"Don?"

Shaking off the memory with a shudder, he eased off Caroline. "You okay?"

"Yes."

Senses on high alert, Don evaluated the threat level. Whatever had exploded had been outside. No one else had entered the room and there hadn't been any subsequent explosions or gunshots. For the moment they were safe. He got his feet beneath him and helped Caroline up.

"Mr. Maddox?"

"Still here," he said with a wry note in his voice.

"What was that?" She clutched his arm as they rose to their feet.

"Not sure." Quickly orienting himself to the dark, he led her to the window and drew back the curtain. Outside, the answer was clear. A huge oak tree a couple yards from the house had been split in two by lightning. Half of the tree's charred remains had landed across the power lines. Sparks danced from the exposed wires torn from their fasteners. The other half of the tree landed in the driveway, effectively blocking the rental car.

Caution traipsed up his spine. What were the chances that lightning would strike that tree causing it to fall in exactly that way? He wanted to inspect the trunk. But that would have to wait until he had Caroline in a secure location.

"I guess the option of leaving before the storm gets worse is off the table," Caroline murmured.

"We can borrow a car."

She made a scoffing noise. "No."

"Roger that." Of course she wouldn't give in that easily.

Horace appeared in the doorway carrying a lit candle. The glow pushed the shadows to the corners. "Mr. Maddox?"

"We're okay here," Elijah answered from the bed. "The others?"

"Everyone is accounted for, sir." He moved all the way into the room to offer Don a pewter candleholder with a thick unlit candle in the center. "Just until the backup generator kicks in."

Don took the holder, tipping it so the wick could touch the lit one in Horace's hand. "Is the power out in the whole house?"

Horace nodded. "Yes. Phone lines down, too. Mrs. Maddox would like to meet you downstairs." From the research, Don knew that must be Abigail Maddox, the wife of Caroline's uncle Samuel.

"I don't think we should leave Mr. Maddox," Caroline said.

From the bed, Elijah said, "Go on, child. I'm tired and need to rest. Mary will be along shortly to keep me company."

"Nothing can be done at the moment," Don stated in a low voice.

"We'll return shortly," Caroline assured her grandfather.

Elijah nodded, but his gaze narrowed to Don. "Keep her safe."

"Of course," Don replied.

They followed Horace downstairs. When they hit the entryway, quick footsteps coming down the hall heralded the arrival of a stylish woman in her early forties wearing tailored black slacks, a pink cashmere sweater and pearls. Her light blond hair was coiffed in an elegant updo. She carried a lit hurricane lamp that added a bright glow to Don's candle.

The woman came to a stop in front of Caroline. "You

look just like Isabella," she said in clipped modulated tones, her eyes assessing.

Hearing of her likeness to Isabella from this woman was different than hearing it from Elijah. There was no sentiment in Abigail's matter-of-fact tone. Just a statement of fact that left Caroline feeling hollow. Elijah had clearly loved his daughter, but there was no indication of warmth or affection coming from her sister-in-law.

"This is Caroline Tully and I'm Don Cavanaugh. Her fiancé," Don said after a tense heartbeat. "And you are?"

"Abigail Maddox." Gesturing to the teens coming down the stairs, she said, "My children, Landon and Lilly. Fraternal twins."

Finding her voice, Caroline said, "Nice to meet you."

"Children, please go out and retrieve…your cousin and her fiancé's travel cases and bring them in," Abigail said.

Caroline's stomach clenched. Cousins. She'd always wanted cousins. Neither of her adopted parents had siblings. But surely they shouldn't be sent out into the storm. Lightning had just struck.

The twins' eyebrows dipped in tandem.

"That's Horace's job, Mother," Landon whined.

Lilly crossed her arms over her chest. "And it's almost time for dinner!"

"The bags can wait," Don said. "It's not safe out there right now."

Impatience flashed across Abigail's face. "Please. It's just a storm. I'm sure you'd like to freshen up before dinner." Her green eyes narrowed on her children. "Do it."

Caroline flinched and exchanged a glance with Don. Aunt Abigail certainly wasn't the warm and fuzzy type.

Landon's shoulders slumped. "Fine." He turned his dark-eyed gaze to Don. "Where are your bags?"

Don held out the keys to the rental. "The trunk."

Landon took the keys and headed toward the door.

His sister stood rooted in place, her hazel gaze studying Caroline. "Why are you here?"

"Lilly, don't be rude. Your granddad invited them. She's here to get to know her family."

The girl snorted her disapproval. "More like she wants his money."

"No, I don't," Caroline blurted quickly. "That's not why I'm here at all." She turned her gaze to Abigail. "I just want to know where I came from."

"Of course, you do," Abigail said, exaggerated understanding lacing her words. "Don't pay them any mind."

Landon pulled open the front door. He glared at his sister.

"Come on, Lilly. You have to help."

Abruptly, Lilly turned and followed her brother out into the rain.

Abigail let out a long-suffering sigh. "I can't wait until they outgrow the surly stage."

Caroline gave a silent sigh of her own. She didn't want to explain her reason for being here any further to her increasingly worrisome relatives.

A middle-age man came out of the adjacent room. "I see our guests have arrived," his deep voice boomed.

"Yes, darling," Abigail said. "Come meet your niece and her young man."

He held out his hand to Don first. "Samuel Maddox."

"Donovan Cavanaugh. Call me Don."

"Good of you to come, Don." Samuel turned his attention to Caroline with a welcoming smile. "I'm so happy to meet you, Caroline."

As she shook his hand, she couldn't help staring into his amber eyes and feeling like she was looking in a mirror. He had raven-colored hair and an olive complexion, much like her own. A blood relative. Her uncle.

"Where are those kids?" Abigail gestured toward the front door with a graceful, bejeweled hand. "Sam, darling, the children are supposed to be bringing in our guests' bags. I'm afraid they may have gotten distracted by the split oak."

The front door burst open on her last word and the twins stumbled in tugging the suitcases behind them. The sound of heavy rain pelting the earth filled the entryway until Lilly slammed the door shut. Pervading humidity made the house damp like a mausoleum. The teens shook their heads, like shaggy dogs, spraying water on everything within reach of the flying droplets.

Abigail said nothing to the twins, though her lips pursed in disapproval. Instead, she turned back to Caroline and Don. "Come, I'll show you to your rooms."

Don handed Caroline the candle, then he grabbed the cases and followed behind. The second story was decorated much like the downstairs—once-elegant furnishings worn bare and shabby. As they passed the open door of one room, Caroline glanced in. Aided by the glow from the candle she carried, she caught the brief impression of cotton-candy-pink walls and ruffles. Most certainly Lilly's domain. Yet the girl didn't seem like the frilly type.

Abigail led them to the end of the hall and stopped

before a closed door. "Mr. Cavanaugh, you'll stay here. Caroline, you will be over here." She moved to the closed door directly across the hall and pushed the door open with a flourish.

Caroline entered to find a beautiful four-poster canopy bed with white linens, a dresser and a vanity and spindle chair. A bench seat stretched beneath the window overlooking the back of the property.

Don set her suitcase on the floor just inside the door. A flash of lightning, lit up the window, making the delicate lace window coverings appear translucent. A second later thunder rumbled. Caroline noticed Don's slight flinch. She was glad they'd made it to the house before the storm had worsened.

"As soon as you come back downstairs we'll serve dinner," Abigail said, clearly unperturbed by the raging weather outside.

Caroline waited until the other woman was out of earshot to whisper to Don, "I hate to think that one of these people wants me and my grandfather dead."

"Your uncle has the most to gain with you out of the way," Don stated. "He'd be the sole heir apparent."

She swallowed back the unease clogging her throat.

Her uncle had greeted her with such warmth. He, like Elijah, had seemed truly glad to see her. Was it all an act? She'd have to use her time here to find the truth. It was the only way she could be safe—and the only way to help her grandfather. Elijah Maddox needed someone to believe him. Someone to protect him. And with her private bodyguard/fake fiancé's help, she was that someone. And maybe while she searched for answers, she'd be able to learn about her mother, as well—

something she'd wanted to do for as long as she could remember.

Despite the apparent danger, she was staying.

Don escorted Caroline to the dining room to find the family already seated at the formal table. Three tall candelabras spaced equal distances apart on the table provided barely adequate light.

Two empty places awaited them. Sensing tension as thick as mortar smoke, Don curbed his desire to whisk Caroline out of the creepy place and instead held out the empty chair next to her uncle at the far end of the table. Landon sat in the chair next to her. Don rounded the table to sit across from Caroline on Samuel's left next to Lilly. Abigail sat at the opposite end of the table. Gold-rimmed china gleamed in the candlelight.

"Lucky for us, dinner was ready before the power went down," Abigail said.

"Horace mentioned there was a back-up generator?" Don asked.

"Yes, in the cellar," Samuel answered. "It's gas powered. I told Horace it could wait until after dinner."

"Dining by candlelight is such a treat," Abigail said. "Don't you agree, Caroline?"

"The candles certainly add ambiance," Caroline replied.

An older woman emerged from a swinging door carrying a steaming platter of vegetables, Horace followed with a platter of sliced roast beef.

"Asparagus? Ugh," Landon whined as the woman placed the green spears on his plate.

"Mind your manners, young man," Samuel said.

Landon shot a venomous glance toward Caroline,

as if she were to blame for the vegetables. Perhaps the kids were not required to eat veggies regularly. Still, the animosity coming off the kid grated on Don. He pinned the boy with a stare until Landon noticed and dropped his gaze to his plate.

"Elijah's illness, was it sudden?" Don asked Samuel, trying to gage his reaction.

A look of sadness passed over the older man's face. "This fall he suffered a nasty bout of pneumonia. According to Dr. Reese, the pneumonia triggered an Addison crisis."

"His body attacked his glands and chewed 'em up like mini, hungry carnivores," Lilly said with relish before stabbing a chunk of meat and devouring it in one bite.

"Gross," Landon complained, dropping his fork with a clatter.

"Lilly, that's enough," Abigail commanded.

"But it's true," she countered with a smirk at her brother.

"Yes, it's true," Samuel said. "Father's body attacked his adrenal glands. It's an autoimmune disease."

Samuel had confirmed what Elijah had said. Don knew very little of the disease but he did know that with proper treatment, people who had it could live fairly normal lives. It didn't make sense that Elijah was still so sick.

"Dr. Reese has tried everything to bring the disease under control, but my father's body isn't cooperating." The sadness in Samuel's eyes appeared genuine. But it could have been a trick of the flickering candle flame.

Don met Caroline's gaze across the table. Candlelight shadowed the contours of her pretty face but he could see her unspoken concern. Was someone slowly killing Elijah, or was he dying a natural death?

As soon as he could, Don would contact Dr. Reese and find out. But the old man wasn't Don's primary concern.

Caroline needed him to protect her. He'd promised. And he never broke a promise.

Even though his gut instinct screamed for him to get Caroline away from the ominous events unfolding around them.

THREE

"My smart phone won't pick up a signal. Not even roaming will latch on long enough to get a call out." Frustration laced each of Don's words. "With the landline down and no wireless service, there's no way to contact the outside world right now."

Inside Caroline's room, he paced in front of the closed door. The light from two brass hurricane lamps elongated his shadow across the wall making him appear like a sinister giant. But Caroline knew a kind spirit lay inside the professional bodyguard.

And a wounded soul.

The thunder clearly unnerved him. Every time an angry clap split through the air, he tensed. His expression took on a haunted appearance making her ache for him. He'd seen battle. The scar on his hand must be a constant reminder of the horrors he'd lived through. Obviously, he carried scars on his psyche, as well.

Everything inside her wanted to comfort him, make him feel safe. How crazy was that? She was the one in danger, but he was the one she wanted to reassure that all was well.

Maybe they needed each other.

The thought left her unbalanced. She didn't want to need anyone. Even a handsome bodyguard. *Especially* a handsome bodyguard. She'd trust him with her safety, but she wasn't ready to trust a man with her heart again. Not after what had happened with Cullen.

A quick check of her cell phone proved fruitless. Frustration throbbed at her temple. "No service for me, either."

Tossing the phone onto the bed, she went to stand by the window overlooking the back of the house. She could barely make out the inky outline of trees in the distance. Rain pelted the window with a rhythmic tap that vibrated through her temple. "Have you noticed there isn't a single Christmas decoration in this house?"

"I hadn't thought about it. I've been a bit distracted what with someone trying to kill you and now the storm trapping us here."

"Right. I'm sure this isn't how you expected to spend your Christmas."

"You hired me to do a job. The date doesn't matter."

A knot formed in her chest. She turned to face him. "You don't celebrate Christmas?"

There was brief hesitation. "I do."

"As an expression of faith?"

His expression shuttered closed. "Yes."

Relief plucked the knot loose. But something in his voice, his guarded eyes, made her think he didn't truly trust God. "But...?"

He shrugged. "War makes you question your beliefs."

She knew firsthand that there were many things that could make a person question their faith. Unexpected death. Betrayal. Anger. She shied away from those thoughts and focused on the warrior in front of her.

She hated to think of the terrors he'd witnessed in a war zone on the other side of the world. The evil men did to each other was sickening. "How long were you in the service?"

"Ten years. I enlisted at eighteen. I've been out for four years."

She glanced at his right hand. In the dim glow of candlelight his scars weren't visible. "That's where you injured your hand."

He flexed his fingers. "Yes. It could have been worse."

"What happened?"

"An IED—an improvised explosive device—used by insurgents in Iraq and Afghanistan."

Her gut clenched. It *could* have been worse. He could have lost his hand—or his life.

A loud bang, like a huge piece of furniture falling somewhere in the house, startled her. "What was that?"

"I'll go find out," Don said and opened the door.

"I'm coming with you." Grabbing the candle, she hurried after him.

They made their way downstairs. There didn't seem to be anyone about. Light shimmered from the far end of a long hallway to the left of the entryway. They headed in that direction. The walls seemed to narrow, darkness and shadows closing in on Caroline as they passed several closed doors and entered the kitchen's arched doorway.

Several lit candles bathed the room in a warm comforting glow. Yellowed, floral wallpaper curled at the edges along the crown molding at the base of the walls.

She imagined her birth mother staring at this same wallpaper. Caroline bet it had looked brighter, cleaner then.

An old-fashioned white gas stove and oven stood next to a state-of-the-art stainless-steel refrigerator. The chipped tile counters hosted modern electric gadgets alongside beat-up older-model appliances. The woman who'd served dinner stood at the tub-style sink, hand washing the gold-rimmed dinnerware they'd eaten from earlier. She was round all over and looked to be on the far side of her golden years. Her short, choppy gray hair curled from the steam rising from the soapy water.

"Excuse me?" Don said.

The woman started and whipped around to face them. A hand went to her throat. "Mercy, I'm likely to have a heart attack, you scared me so."

"We're sorry," Caroline said with a smile.

"We heard a loud noise, is everything okay?" Don asked.

The woman shrugged. "Must've been one of the kids slamming a door. They're always slamming the doors."

Caroline glanced at Don. He looked as doubtful as she felt.

"I'm Caroline and this is Don. Are you Mary?"

The older woman nodded. Wary shadows darkened the irises of her light brown eyes. "I know who you are. You come from up north. You're Ms. Isabella's daughter."

"You knew my mother?"

"Yes, ma'am. I helped raise both of Mr. Elijah and Mrs. Mauve's children. I help now with Mrs. Abigail's twins, too." She shook her head. "Those two are like mad cats in a pillow case dawn to dusk."

The description of the teens sparked a bit of humor in Caroline. Abigail had her hands full for sure. Sobering, Caroline asked, "What can you tell me about my mother?"

A sorrow-filled smile touched the older woman's face. "She was a lovely child. Quiet. Obedient." Mary turned back to the sink.

"Do you know where Samuel is?" Don asked, tension coming off him in waves.

"Most likely with the missus in the parlor or upstairs in their rooms. They have the whole west side of the second floor."

"And Horace? Where is he?"

She cocked her head. "I figure you might try outside. A tree fell across the driveway."

"Yes, we saw that," Caroline said.

Lightning zigzagged across the sky, the bright light visible through the kitchen window. Thunder rattled the glass. Don inhaled sharply. Caroline touched his arm, aware of how the storm was affecting him. His muscle jumped beneath her hand. She had a feeling it wasn't the weather but something more that was causing such intense reactions to the thunder and lightning. Flashbacks to his time in the military?

"Do storms like these happen often here?" Caroline asked.

Picking up a dish towel, Mary faced them as she dried a plate and stacked it neatly on the counter. "Occasionally. This one here's not so bad. Other than the lightning hitting so close to the house." She seemed unfazed by the narrow margin of disaster that could have been. "And there is a storm cellar in case a tornado kicks up."

Caroline blinked. Visions of being swept away like Dorothy in the *Wizard of Oz* flashed in her mind. "Tornado?"

They definitely weren't in Boston anymore.

"One hasn't touched down in the valley in years," Mary said.

Well, that was some comfort. Still she couldn't help but imagine flying cows and monkeys.

"We should go find your uncle," Don prompted.

He was right, but she had more questions for Mary. "I'd like to stay here."

For a moment, he contemplated her request, his gaze darting to Mary and back, before slowly nodding. "Stay put. I'll be right back."

"I will," she assured him. He left, taking a candle with him.

Mary eyed her curiously. "You want to talk to me, miss?"

"About my mother."

Mary nodded and resumed her dishwashing. "What would you like to know?"

"You said as a child she was quiet, obedient. What was she like as an adult?"

"Proud. Stubborn. Full of dreams."

So that was where Caroline's streak of stubbornness came from. Interesting. What else did they have in common? "What did she dream of?"

Mary bustled about, putting the dinnerware in a cabinet. "Not my place to say, ma'am."

"Please, I need to know."

Mary pressed her lips together for a moment. Caroline was afraid she'd refuse to answer. She held her breath.

"She wanted to be a lawyer. She'd gone off to that fancy school to study law. Mr. Elijah was none too happy about it."

Remembering Elijah's comment, Caroline asked, "What did Elijah want her to do?"

"Be a proper Southern woman. Marry well, have children."

She'd had a child. But she'd given her up. Why? And what about marriage—what had been her relationship with Caroline's father? "Do you know who my father is?"

Mary shook her head and turned away, but not before Caroline saw a flash of something—Anguish? Regret?—in her eyes.

Quick footsteps coming down the hall prevented Caroline from probing for more information. She turned as Abigail glided into the kitchen, holding a pewter candlestick with a deep purple candle attached. The candle's flame made Abigail's complexion look sallow.

"Here you are, Caroline. What on earth are you doing in the kitchen? Let Mary get her work done in peace." She tsked and took Caroline's arm. "Don and Samuel are outside helping Horace with the tree. Come, let us get better acquainted."

Caroline hesitated. She'd told Don she wouldn't leave the kitchen, but how did she refuse to accompany her aunt without being rude? She sent Mary an apologetic smile and allowed her aunt to lead her from the room. She hoped Don would understand.

Halfway down the hall, Abigail stopped and pushed open a door. "Here we go."

The room was warm and well lit with at least a dozen

candles on the curved-legged tables and on top of the square upright piano in the corner. The twins sat on an ornate antique sofa in the middle of the room. The furniture style was much more Victorian than Federal like most of the other pieces in the house. Lilly had her nose in a book and Landon hunched over a half-finished jigsaw puzzle on the coffee table. There was no television, no computer. Actually, she hadn't seen any electronics since arriving, even though there had been electricity available to run them, then.

Taking a seat in a Queen Anne–style chair, Caroline asked, "Is there a computer I can use when the power comes back on?"

Lilly snorted without looking up from her book. Caroline read the spine—*Moby Dick*. Interesting. Required reading for school, or pleasure?

"Very unladylike," Abigail said with censure in her tone. Her gaze swung back to Caroline. "Elijah is very much against bringing anything into the house that corrupts the mind."

"But don't the twins need a computer for homework?"

Landon slid a dark glance her way. "Our tutors don't require them."

"You don't attend school?"

For a moment no one said anything, then Abigail sighed. "Elijah prefers to have the children's teachers come to the house."

"Does Uncle Samuel have a computer?"

"At his office in town." Abigail settled on a stool at the piano. Her nimble fingers danced over the keys playing a pretty melody that Caroline didn't recognize.

"I don't seem to get any cell service here," Caroline

said. "Would any of you happen to have a cell phone I could use?"

Lilly lowered her book and glared. "We don't have cell phones, either."

Her contentious expression echoed her tone. Obviously she felt deprived. Caroline couldn't blame her. In this day and age, it seemed archaic not to have a cell phone or computer. Switching gears, Caroline said, "Tomorrow's Christmas. I noticed you don't have a tree or anything."

Abigail faltered, her fingers hitting discordant notes.

The twins stared at Caroline with widened eyes. She could see the longing in their young faces.

Finally, Abigail turned to face her. "Elijah doesn't believe in Christmas."

"Doesn't believe in the commercialism, or doesn't believe in God?"

Abigail gave a noncommittal shrug. "Both, I suppose."

A deep sadness invaded Caroline to know her grandfather didn't believe in God. Having faith was such an integral part of her life. Granted, her adoptive parents raised her in a Christian environment, but as an adult she'd chosen faith over anything else this world had to offer, even if she felt distant from God since Cullen's death. "I saw a Bible on the entryway table. Whom does that belong to?"

"It was Mauve's."

Mauve Maddox, Caroline's grandmother. Caroline wondered what she'd think of this situation. "And you? Do you believe in God?"

Abigail's gaze shifted back to the piano. "I don't know what I believe."

Caroline looked to the twins. They shared a glance, then shrugged before resuming their activities.

Apparently Elijah held the family in a tight grip. It was hard to equate the frail man lying upstairs who'd seemed genuinely concerned for Caroline's safety with the picture of a stern authoritarian being painted by his family.

The door to the parlor swung open. Don burst in, a flashlight in his hand, and halted abruptly, his gaze zeroing in on Caroline.

Samuel entered, stepping around him.

"There she is," Samuel said, his gaze on Caroline as he moved to stand behind the sofa. "I told you she was fine."

Caroline winced. Concern deepened the color of Don's eyes to steely cobalt, reminding her of the danger waiting to strike. She'd let down her guard. Suddenly she felt drained. And it wasn't even eight o'clock in the evening. She rose from the chair. "It's been a long day. I'll say good-night now."

Abigail moved to stand next to Samuel. With the twins sitting on the sofa in front of the couple, they looked liked a Norman Rockwell family. A shiver of apprehension slid down Caroline's spine. Could this idyllic scene be hiding something sinister?

"Good night, Caroline. Sleep well."

Caroline doubted that would happen. One of these people might want her dead. But the question was which one?

Don leaned against the doorjamb of her room. "You left the kitchen."

His heart beat too rapidly. When he'd returned to the

kitchen and found the room empty, panic had drained the blood from his brain and sent his heart rate into overdrive.

Number One Rule of Protection—never leave your protectee unguarded.

But dragging Caroline out into the storm hadn't been an option, either. She'd be too exposed, with too many places for a bad guy to take a shot at her. He had been sure she was safer inside with Mary.

Except neither Mary nor Caroline had been where he'd left them when he returned.

Caroline grimaced. "I know. Sorry. Aunt Abigail came in and didn't give me much choice."

When Samuel suggested Caroline was with his family in the parlor, Don had nearly trampled over the older man getting into the room. Seeing Caroline safe had eased but did not erase the constriction in his chest. Failing to protect her was not an option.

Especially after examining the tree trunk and determining lightning hadn't been the cause of the tree splitting in half so neatly. There'd been no mistaking the burn pattern of an explosive device, nor the bits of metal embedded in the thick wood where its hole had been made with a spike.

"The tree wasn't hit by lightning," he stated baldly.

She paled in the candlelight. "What?"

"Someone deliberately destroyed that tree with an explosive. It was set to fall exactly where it did—blocking us in and cutting off the power."

She sat on the bed. "The same bomber who tried to kill me in Boston?"

"That would be a fair assumption. Reconsider leaving."

Shaking her head, she said, "I'm considering it all the time. But where would I go? The bomber found me in Boston once already. Am I supposed to hide for the rest of my life? No. I'm staying here until I get some answers. Besides, I can't leave until we're sure Elijah's safe."

Stubborn. Courageous. Beautiful. He tried not to admire her but he did.

"First thing in the morning I'll contact the local law enforcement."

Her grateful smile hit him in the gut. She had such pretty features he could stare at her for hours. Time to retreat.

"I'll leave my door cracked open," he said, reluctant to leave her again, even though propriety demanded he did. "Make sure you lock this door."

"Any idea when they'll get the generator working?"

"Not until they get some gas to run it." He still couldn't believe they had no fuel for the thing. "With the landline phone not working, we'll have to wait until we can go into town to pick some up."

She rose and glided to a stop in front of him. "I asked Abigail if there was a cell phone I could use. She said Elijah doesn't allow any electronics in the house."

The warm glow of the candlelight bathed her face and reflected in her gold-flecked eyes. He struggled to stay on topic. "Samuel said the same thing. Though he confessed he has a laptop in his quarters that he uses for his work."

Her eyes brightened impossibly more. "That's good. Will he let you use it? Maybe we could contact Dr. Reese?"

"He will." His mouth quirked. "Through the internet

since the phones aren't working. Once the electricity is restored."

Disappointment turned the corners of her mouth down. "Wow. It's like we're trapped in some time warp."

"Exactly." Being so cut off from the rest of the world left Don feeling uneasy. Especially with an assassin on the loose. "In the morning, we'll drive to town and talk to Dr. Reese in person."

"Tomorrow's Christmas Day. You think the doctor will be in his office?"

"No." He blew out a breath. "I guess we'll have to wait until the day after to talk to him unless we can find his emergency contact number."

He didn't want to wait. The quicker they figured out if there was a connection between the bomber's attacks and Elijah's illness, the quicker the culprit could be found, and his protection detail could end. "But the local police will be on duty. They don't take holidays off. We need to keep them informed and ready to act."

Anxiety tightened the corners of her mouth. "Thank you."

"That's what you're paying me for."

Her gaze dropped. "True. Some Christmas, huh?" A pensive, sad expression crossed her face. "Abigail said Elijah doesn't let them celebrate Christmas."

He arched an eyebrow. "Not everyone does."

"I know not everyone believes in God or celebrates Christmas, but I've seen evidence of faith in the house. Elijah has a cross hanging in his room, and there's a Bible in the entryway that has clearly seen some use. I feel bad for the kids."

"They have everything they need," Don said. They

had more than he'd had as a kid. He'd have traded every Christmas present he'd ever received to have his father return.

"I suppose you're right. A roof over their heads, food on the table. Tutors who come to them. But where's the joy?" She rubbed her arms.

"Cold?"

"A little."

Without thinking through the consequences, he wrapped her in his embrace. She snuggled closer, sending his blood racing. He told himself he was acting the part of her fiancé, in case one of the family members happened to walk by the open door. But a niggling voice cautioned that he liked holding her a little too much.

Leaning back to look up at him, she said, "I'm sad for this family. They seem so oppressed."

"Makes you wonder, doesn't it?"

"Wonder?"

"Maybe Elijah is right that someone's killing him. Maybe someone's tired of living under his thumb."

"Oh. Right. I see where you're going with that." She shivered. He tightened his hold. "But no one deserves to be murdered. If Uncle Samuel and his family don't like living here, why don't they leave?"

Don shrugged. "The old man holds the purse strings." Which was more than enough motive to do away with Elijah. And Caroline. To do that, though, they'd have to go through him first.

"I want to talk to Elijah," she said. "He should let these kids have a merry Christmas if only to bring some fun and joy to this gloomy house."

The determined note in her voice raised alarms in

Don. "Are you sure you want to interfere? Can't you wait until we know more about him and his condition?"

She extracted herself from his arms. "Yes, I'm sure. And no, I can't wait."

She pushed past him and headed down the hall toward the patriarch's room. Don had no choice but to follow. As her bodyguard and as her fake fiancé. He only hoped she knew what she was doing.

FOUR

Caroline knocked once, and then entered without waiting for an invitation. Light pooled in a small circle around the bedside table from a battery-powered lamp. Elijah watched them as they approached. He seemed to have shrunken further since she'd last seen him.

Spying an ornate chair in the corner, she dragged it forward. Don quickly lifted the chair and set it near the bed for her. Giving him a grateful smile, she sat down. Her heart pounded in her chest. She shouldn't be afraid to talk to this old man about God. She'd gone on mission trips to Third World countries and helped out at homeless shelters in downtown Boston. Talking to strangers about their need for God had never made her feel as insecure as she felt right now. For some reason she wasn't sure how to proceed.

Don placed a hand on her shoulder. She touched his hand and gained strength from him.

She went for the straightforward approach. "Mr. Maddox, why won't you let your family celebrate Christmas? Even if you don't believe in God or even the commercialism of the presents and such, it's unfair not to let your family choose for themselves."

His eyes widened, and then narrowed. "Is that what they told you? That I don't believe?"

"Yes."

He snorted. "Idiots. I believe in God. And I know that He is punishing me." Turning away, he said in a tortured, angry tone, "God took Isabella away because I didn't take good enough care of her. You can't ask me to celebrate Him."

Elijah's words hit her like a fist to the stomach. "Isabella was murdered by an intruder. How can you blame yourself?"

Elijah's eyes misted. "I didn't protect her."

"I don't understand."

"I should have kept her from going off to college." Elijah's voice held self-recrimination. "She refused to come home for the summer that year. The last time I saw her was the Christmas before she died. We had an ugly argument."

Anguish squeezed Caroline's lungs. No wonder he held this family in such a tight grip. She reached out to touch Elijah's hand. "God didn't take her away. A criminal did that. God's not punishing you for letting her live her life."

"Then why? Why didn't God protect her?"

Hurting for Isabella and for the man who carried her death like a scar on his heart, Caroline sought the right words. "We live in a fallen world. I know that sounds trite, but it's true nonetheless. This wasn't God's plan. He loved Isabella, just as He loves you. He wouldn't want you to take the blame for someone's evil deed."

Elijah squeezed her hand. "You have your mother's fire." For a long moment he stared at her then gestured toward the bedside table. "Open the drawer."

She did as he asked. Inside she found a small Bible, pen and paper. But Caroline's gaze was drawn to the two other items in the drawer. A pair of hospital bracelets.

Tears clogged her throat as she lifted the larger bracelet. She read Isabella Maddox's name and the date. Caroline's birth date. The small bracelet read Baby Girl Maddox and had the same date.

"After Isabella's death, her things were boxed and shipped home. I never looked through them until this past October. The anniversary of her death. She'd have been forty-eight this year." A tear slipped down his face.

Caroline's heart squeezed tight. "This is how you discovered she'd had a child."

He nodded, then looked away. "You'll find more of your mother's belongings in a trunk in the attic."

Affection for this gruff old man unfurled in her chest. "Thank you. What a wonderful Christmas gift."

Elijah gave her a half smile full of sadness. "Mauve loved to decorate the house for Christmas. And gifts… Oh, she'd be downright giddy giving the perfect present to everyone she loved. She always said we gave gifts because God gave us the best gift, His Son." Elijah blinked back more tears. "She would've liked you. You speak your mind."

"When did Mauve pass on?"

"Three years after Isabella's death. Massive coronary."

Sympathy pinched Caroline's heart. "You miss her."

"I do. Especially…" Elijah's gaze drifted toward the window as if he were seeing something in the past.

Then he shifted his eyes back to Caroline's face. "There are Christmas decorations in the attic, as well."

Surprise washed over her. She leaned in and kissed his withered cheek. "Thank you. God bless you."

"No, God bless you, child, for coming here to see a dying old man you've never met." His gaze jumped to Don. "You keep her safe, you hear?"

"Believe me, sir, I intend to."

Elijah nodded.

A light rapping sounded at the door.

"Excuse me?" Mary stepped in. "It's time for Mr. Maddox's medications."

In one hand she held a plastic cup filled with four round white pills, and a glass of water in the other.

"What are those?" Don asked, easing closer.

"Florinef and Cortef for his Addison's."

Caroline stood and moved out of the way for Mary to hand Elijah the pills and water. He quickly swallowed the medication.

Mary took the glass from Elijah and set it on the bedside table. "Are you comfortable, Mr. Maddox?"

"Yes, Mary. Dinner, as always, was delicious."

She smiled. "I'm just glad it was all cooked before the tree fell." She turned to leave. "Ring if you need anything."

Elijah nodded and she left.

"Ring?" Caroline asked.

He pointed with a bony finger to the small bell on the table then pointed upward. "Mary's room is there."

"There's a third floor with rooms?" Caroline had assumed only the attic was overhead.

He nodded as his eyelids drooped. "The attic takes

up half the third floor while their quarters take up the other half."

"How long has Mary worked for you?" Don asked.

Caroline shot Don a curious look.

"She's been with the family since she was a child. Her mamma was my grandparents' cook. Mary took over when Constance passed on, just a few years after she married Horace, and brought him to work for us, too." His words slurred at the end as sleepiness laced his tone.

Seeing Elijah's fatigue prompted Caroline to take Don's hand. "We'll let you rest now. We plan to talk with your doctor as soon as possible."

Elijah's eyelids fluttered. "Be safe." Caroline tugged Don out of the room.

"What do you think?" she asked in a soft whisper when they were in the hall.

His flashlight created a circle of light on the faded carpet. "Not sure what to think."

"I'd like to go to the attic." She glanced around, wondering which closed door led upstairs.

Lilly emerged out of the shadows, her face obscured by inky darkness. "Why do you want to go to the attic?"

Stilling the momentary jump of her heart rate, Caroline answered, "Mr. Maddox said we could decorate for Christmas."

She couldn't yet bring herself to call him her grandfather out loud.

"It's a little late for that now," Lilly muttered.

"It's never too late for Christmas." Though she supposed for the teenager, Christmas was about presents and Santa Claus, not about the birth of Jesus. Still,

Caroline wanted to bring some Christmas joy into this gloomy house.

The girl shrugged. "Door's at the other end of the hall."

"We could sure use your help," Caroline said.

"No." As quietly as she'd appeared she left. Don raised the flashlight on her retreating back. She entered her bedroom and disappeared inside without a backward glance.

Don mimicked the girl's shrug and Caroline had to stifle an unexpected snicker.

They found the door and took the narrow staircase upward. At the top another door waited. They tried the handle. Locked.

"Maybe Samuel or Abigail has the key." Frustration laced Caroline's words.

They headed back downstairs and found the couple in the parlor. Landon still worked at his puzzle. Samuel sat by the window reading a book while Abigail played the piano. All three looked up as they entered the room.

Abigail lifted her hands from the ivory keys. "Did my playing disturb you?"

"No," Caroline quickly assured her. "This house is amazingly quiet."

Samuel set his book aside. "Yes. They don't build houses like this anymore." The pride lacing his tone belied the condition of the house.

Was Uncle Samuel killing his father so he could gain control of the family's wealth? Was he behind the threat to Caroline's life? Caroline tried to keep the suspicions from showing on her face.

"Do you have a key to the attic?" Don asked.

Abigail rose from the bench. "Why on earth would you want to go in there? It's dusty and full of cobwebs."

"Mr. Maddox gave us permission," Don said.

"He said we could decorate for Christmas," Caroline added.

Abigail smiled but not before Caroline noted the flash of something—disapproval, maybe—in her green eyes. "It seems silly to decorate now considering we'd just have to pack everything away day after tomorrow."

Caroline wouldn't be dissuaded. There was more she wanted from the attic than decorations. "And he said I would find some of my mother's things."

"Ah." Abigail's expression softened. "Of course."

"There are indeed some of Isabella belongings," Samuel said. "Let me show you where we keep the key."

A swirl of confusion ignited in Caroline's mind. Abigail and Samuel's understanding and acceptance of her desire for her mother's things appeared genuine.

Samuel led them to the kitchen. He opened the pantry door and lifted a key from a hook mounted on the wall. "My father told you about Isabella?"

Caroline nodded; she still wasn't ready to let the impact of her birth mother's death hit her.

"Such a tragedy. Broke our hearts."

The genuine pain in his voice touched Caroline. Could he really be the one behind the attempts on her life? "Were you two close?"

"She was three years older than me. I thought the world of her. Isabella could light up a room with her smile." A wistful expression crossed his face. "And her laugh. She had the best laugh." His expression fell. "There hasn't been much laughter in this house since she left."

Caroline's heart squeezed with sympathy. "I'm so sorry."

Seeming to shake off his melancholy, Samuel handed her a brass lever-lock-style key. "This will open the attic door."

He walked away and rejoined his family in the parlor.

Caroline sighed and closed her hand over the key commonly referred to as a skeleton key because it resembled a skeletal figure. "They're still hurting even after all this time."

"Isabella's case was never closed," Don reminded her.

Her death remained an open wound for this family.

A killer roamed free.

Caroline shivered with dread.

Would she be another victim?

With the antique key in her hand, Caroline and Don returned to the top of the narrow staircase. The key fit easily into the lock, and with a soft click, the door opened. Caroline stepped out of the way to allow Don to enter first. The flame of the candle she held danced as he moved past. A second later, he motioned for her to join him.

She breathed in musty, stale air and coughed. Her gaze tracked the light from Don's candle as he swept the beam across the large space that ran half the length of the house. Thick cobwebs hung from the rafters. More antique furniture, trunks of various sizes and cardboard boxes labeled with neat script were stowed at the far end of the attic.

"You don't think there are spiders up here do you?"

Caroline set down the candle she carried on a book-shelf, careful to make sure nothing was close enough to catch fire.

"Where there are cobwebs…" He shrugged. "Sorry, I doubt these came out of a can."

She laughed. "You're right. It's an attic. Most likely there are spiders."

Despite her attempt at appearing unaffected, a shud-der of distaste worked through her. Ever since she was eight, creepy crawly things freaked her out. She'd run through a spider web with the spider still in it. For months after she was tormented with the sensation of something crawling along her scalp.

A shiver hit her. She combed a hand through her hair. But she refused to be afraid with Don here. She'd have to shoo away any creepers and step on any ugly bugs herself. But she wasn't sure she'd could stomach picking out any spiders from her hair.

"Would have been nice if the old man had said which trunk," Don commented. He set the flashlight on its flat end so it acted like a lamp, providing a good measure of light. "I'll find the Christmas stuff while you check the trunks."

Cautiously, she opened the closest trunk, keeping an eye out for any eight-legged inhabitants. Lifting the lid dislodged a film of dust. She sneezed. Inside the trunk were neatly stacked household items. She touched an old washboard. There was so much history in this house, in these trunks. But she was thankful for modern conve-niences that made things like the washboard obsolete.

The next trunk contained musty woman's clothes. Matronly. Must be Mauve Maddox's. Another trunk held Mississippi State University memorabilia. Judging by the dates, they belonged to Uncle Samuel. Caroline opened three more trunks filled with more clothes and items from bygone eras before she finally discovered the one she sought.

"Found it," she breathed out after opening the lid. Don crouched by her side.

The trunk was ornately carved with running horses and swirling flowers and vines. Inside were frilly dresses, a pressed gardenia. One of Caroline's favorite blooms. A book of poetry by Tennyson. And a stack of greeting cards tied neatly together with a faded purple ribbon.

She untied the bow and carefully inspected the cards. Most were signed by Isabella's mother, but a few were signed by Elijah in a hard, looping scrawl. "Birthday cards."

Caroline returned the note cards to the trunk and picked up a thick green bound book with a large *T* surrounded by a wave in the middle of the cover.

"What's that?" Don asked, leaning closer.

Awareness shimmied over her. The companionable way they were working together pleased her. She flipped open the cover. "Tulane yearbook for 1983. Isabella's first year of college."

She quickly found the pages with the university freshman dorm group pictures. Holding the book at an angle to capture the light, she scanned the faces and the names. Isabella Maddox sat center, a wide smile on her face. She looked young and carefree. For a moment, tears blurred Caroline's vision.

"She was pretty," Don commented over her shoulder. "You do look like her."

Pleased by the compliment, she closed the book

and blinked back the tears. She'd peruse it later in private. Caroline was curious to see what clubs and activities her mother had been involved in. Setting the yearbook aside, she reached in the trunk and pulled out a leather-bound journal. She flipped it open. Neatly penned words filled the lined pages.

"Isabella's journal." Her throat tightened. "Maybe I'll find out who my father was."

Don put one hand out to draw her attention and put a finger to his lips. She raised an eyebrow.

"Did you hear that?" he whispered.

She hadn't heard anything. A tremor of alarm traced her spine.

"Someone was on the stairs." He stealthily made his way toward the stairwell.

The slam of a door echoed in the attic's rafters. Caroline flinched. Don hurried through the open door at the top of the stairs.

He returned a moment later. "The door to the hall is locked."

"Someone locked us in here?"

"Looks that way."

Unnerved, she handed him the key. "Do you think this will work?"

"Worth a try."

His flashlight cut to the doorway. Curling smoke rose from the stairwell filling the attic.

Caroline froze. Panic pounded in her head. "Don!"

Someone had set the house on fire!

Fear tightened a noose around Don's neck.

"Get down!" He tackled Caroline to the floor, beneath the smoke.

They were trapped.

Heart-pounding terror flooded through him. He labored to breathe.

Flashes of the last time he'd been under heavy artillery fire bombarded his mind. All around him the smell of death.

"Don?"

The echoing screams of dying soldiers rang in his ears.

"Cavanaugh!"

He started, returning to the present, to the woman pinned beneath him. "You okay?"

"Squished. *You* okay?"

He made a noncommittal noise in this throat and eased off her. Aiming the flashlight's beam toward the smoke billowing out of the stairwell, he expected to see golden flames licking the wall, but the beam of light reflected nothing but a rainbow-hued haze. He frowned. What in the world? "Stay here."

Covering his mouth and nose with the end of his shirt, he inspected the colorful cloud. The nauseating smell of saltpeter burned his nostrils, reminding him of childhood summers. "The house isn't on fire. The colored smoke's from a Fourth of July firework. A smoke bomb."

"Is it poisonous?"

"Not necessarily. However without some ventilation we'll likely get sick from inhaling the smoke." He motioned toward her lit candle. "Put that out. Just in case." He didn't think the fumes would ignite but he preferred to err on the side of caution.

That was his job.

"We're going to have to wait for the smoke to evaporate before we try going down the stairwell."

They needed fresh air. He shut the attic door. That lessened the incoming flow of the noxious fumes. He swung the beam of light around the walls and spied an octagonal window up high at the far end of the room. "We've got to get to that window."

"How about stacking the trunks on top of each other?" Caroline suggested.

"Good idea."

Working quickly, they emptied several trunks, then stacked them high. Don climbed up to the window. Covering his hand with a thick fabric he'd found in a trunk, he broke the glass. Fresh, moisture-laden air poured in. He gestured toward her. "It's stable enough for us both to climb on up."

He helped Caroline to the top. They stood pressed together, their faces turned to the window.

"You didn't answer me, *are* you okay?" she asked, concern underscoring her words.

Taking a full breath and slowly letting it out, he nodded. "Yes. I can protect you."

"I'm not questioning your ability." She touched his arm, drawing his gaze to where her warmth seeped through her shirt sleeve. "I sensed something happening to you, in you. PTSD?"

Perceptive. "Yes. I suffer occasional bouts of post-traumatic stress disorder. Not anything for you to worry about." He hadn't meant for his voice to take on such a hard edge. "I can do my job."

Slipping her hand away, she said, "Good to know." She fell silent.

A round of frenzied barking floated in from the busted window.

"Where do you suppose those dogs are?" she asked.

Grateful for the change in subject, he answered, "Samuel has a kennel at the back of the property. Hunting dogs, he said."

She coughed. "This is not how I imagined my first night here. Especially on Christmas Eve."

"Hey, it'll be okay. The pyrotechnic gems will burn themselves out soon enough." He hoped. Then he'd figure out a way to escape the confines of the attic. And confront whoever locked them inside. He was pretty sure he knew who was responsible. The fireworks seemed like a childish—teenage—prank.

Not nearly as serious as the attempt on Caroline's life in Boston or the explosive that felled the tree outside.

"What would you usually be doing on Christmas Eve?" he asked.

She sighed, the sound making it obvious she missed her family. "My parents and I would attend the early evening service at our church, then home for Swedish meatballs and lingonberry sauce, mashed potatoes and green beans with slivered almonds. And then we'd watch a movie. Either *White Christmas* or *It's a Wonderful Life*."

"That sounds nice."

"It is. What about you? What is a typical Christmas Eve like for you?"

He didn't have the Norman Rockwell kind of upbringing that she did. "It depends on what assignment I'm on. Last year I was in California on Christmas Eve providing security for a celebrity."

"Really? Who?"

The curiosity in her voice was cute. "Sorry. Not allowed to give out any information on clients."

She pretended to pout. "Come on, you can confide in me. I won't say a word to anyone."

"Against the rules."

"You like rules?"

"I do. Keeps things simple and predictable."

"But doesn't leave much room for spontaneity and fun."

He shrugged. "Maybe not, but sticking to the rules can save lives." And guaranteed he didn't end up a loser. Like his father.

Caroline slanted him a glance. "Can I ask you something?"

Wariness tensed his shoulder muscles. "Sure."

"Are you married?"

He choked on a laugh. "Now how could I be your fiancé and be married?"

"Fake fiancé," she reminded him. "I really don't know that much about you."

"Right." Though part of him wanted to erase the pretense. He must have inhaled too much of the colorful fog. "No, I'm not married."

"Ever been close to tying the knot?"

He cut her a quick glance. Light from the flashlight he held danced across the contours of her pretty face. The question played in his head and he contemplated the best answer.

"You don't have to tell me," she said quickly, shifting away, obviously taking his hesitation as reluctance. "Just seems something a fiancé would know about her intended."

He couldn't argue that logic. "Once, briefly."

"What happened?" Curiosity laced her words.

The truth rose but he quickly batted it back. Instead he went with the easier answer, the less complicated and revealing truth. "We were seventeen."

"Ah. Too young for sure."

He nodded, again taking the easy path.

She yawned, making adorable little noises that sent his blood pounding. Mist from the rain coming through the broken window swirled around them.

"You're tired." He drew her down to sit on the top trunk. "You need to rest."

The energy seemed to drain out of her. She sagged like a rag doll.

Afraid she'd topple off their perch, he eased her close and tucked her head beneath his chin. She stiffened in his arms, but then relaxed, her warmth pressing into him, making his heart thud in booming beats he was sure she could feel through the fabric of his shirt.

Nice job sticking to the rules, Cavanaugh, his conscience mocked.

The flashlight's beam dimmed. The battery was running out. He flipped it off.

"To conserve what power is left," he explained when she lifted her head.

He held himself still, waiting. Expecting her to move away from him. Needing her to move away from him.

She returned her head to his shoulder. She let out a little wistful breath and snuggled in ever so slightly.

He closed his eyes, allowing himself to savor the moment for what it was. A moment in time that would end once they broke free of the attic.

FIVE

"You know I was engaged once, right?" Caroline asked quietly.

Don sucked in a breath. Empathy tightened his throat, making his voice sound constricted. He knew her fiancé had died. "Kris mentioned it."

"Cullen." The sadness in her tone stabbed at him. She still grieved. "We met at Boston University our senior year. We dated for four years before we became engaged."

"How long has he been gone?" he asked gently.

"Two years this New Year's Day. He went skiing in Berkshire East, and had a bad fall."

The subtle change in her tone was unmistakable. Anger.

"I didn't want him to go, and we fought about it that morning on the phone. He was supposed to come to New Hampshire and spend the day with my family. But he chose not to. Our last words were said in anger."

Don winced, hurting for her. She'd not only lost the man she loved, but their last words had been part of an argument. He could hear the anguish in her tone, feel it in her body. Was the undertone of anger directed at herself or at Cullen? Don soothed a hand down her back. "Don't remember the anger. Remember the good times, the love you shared."

"Sometimes it hurts too much to do that."

His heart squeezed tight recognizing the truth in her words. "I understand."

"You do?" Curiosity echoed in her voice. "Who did you lose?"

"My mom. To pancreatic cancer."

Without lifting her head from his shoulder, she placed her hand over his heart, burning a hole right through him. "I'm so sorry. That's a bad one."

"Yeah, it was." He fought the memories, the sorrow. "I was in Iraq when I got the call. I returned home to care for her. She went fast once the diagnosis came in."

"Were you close?"

He thought about the question. "Not sure *close* is the right word. We had a strained relationship. She always said I was too much like my father—and not in a good way."

She drew back. "Is it just you and your dad now?"

Her question poked at an old wound, one he wanted to go away. "No. My dad took off when I was eleven."

She made an anguished noise and flexed her fingers against his chest. Her touch was protective and soothing and making him ache something fierce.

"I didn't know."

"How could you? It's not something I like to talk about." Maybe it was the anonymity of the dark, the warmth of holding Caroline so close, or just the need to speak that made him add, "He was a loser. Couldn't hack the responsibility of a family. Left us to fend for ourselves."

"You never heard from him again?"

He swallowed back the anger, the hurt. "No. Never. As a kid I cried out to God to bring my father back. As an adult I'd cried out to God to heal my mom as she lay dying. My prayers had fallen on deaf ears."

"No. Just because you didn't get the answer you wanted doesn't mean God wasn't listening. Sometimes silence means no."

"I suppose you're right. I doubt I'd have any faith left if not for the times I'd felt God's presence while in the heat of a war zone."

"The world isn't all bad, though," she said, slipping her arms around him in a comforting embrace. "There's beauty and goodness, too. God is present all the time."

"I'll need to remember that."

She tilted her head. His breath caught and held as she placed a gentle kiss on his jaw, igniting a longing that jolted through him.

"Caroline."

Her name came out a warning, a craving. Her small hands gripped his head and drew him close until she found his mouth. Lost in the moment, he returned the kiss, reveling in her warm and pliant lips. So inviting. The kiss deepened to a threatening level. Alarm sirens went off in his head. They were marching toward disaster. Each second brought them closer to a land mine that would disintegrate them both.

He broke the kiss. The sounds of their ragged breathing roared in his ears. Slowly he disengaged from her with an apology on his lips. "That shouldn't have happened. I overstepped myself. I broke the rules. It won't happen again."

Her silence scored him. "Caroline?"

"Can we get out of here now?" she asked.

His heart twisted in his chest. He'd broken Rule Number Three—Keep Your Hands to Yourself.

Angry at himself, he flipped on the flashlight. The weak beam dispelled the shadows and accentuated the hurt on Caroline's face. His heart squeezed the breath from his lungs. The last thing he ever wanted to do was hurt her.

But he had.

He was supposed to protect her, not kiss her.

He'd made a tactical error. She was vulnerable right now, still grieving her fiancé, reeling from learning of her birth mother and her Mississippi family. He'd added to her pain by allowing his attraction to complicate her life.

He needed to get his head on straight, dial down his attraction and remember his duty. Protect his client from all danger.

Including him.

She climbed down without another word.

He followed. Though the stench from the smoke bombs lingered in the air, he could breathe easily enough. He went to the shelves and rummaged around.

"What are you looking for?" Caroline asked.

"A screwdriver."

"I think I saw one." She moved to one of the rounded-top trunks and dug inside. Holding up a Philips head, she asked, "Will this work?"

He closed his hand over hers. For a moment neither spoke. She tugged her hand free, leaving him with the screwdriver.

"Caroline—"

She held up her hand. "Please. Just forget it."

Forgetting how she felt in his arms, tasted on his lips, was not going to happen anytime soon. But dwelling on his infraction wouldn't get them out of the attic. He went to work at removing the locked doorknob to the hall. The thing came readily apart.

"Wait!" Caroline headed back up the stairwell to the attic. "We forgot the Christmas decorations."

She still wanted to decorate the house. Even after being smoked out. Amazing.

Caroline arranged the nativity set on the large round table in the entryway. The little porcelain figurines depicting shepherds, animals, Mary and Joseph and baby Jesus felt cold to the touch. Much like how her heart felt.

What had she been thinking to initiate that kiss?

She slanted a glance to the archway between the library and the entryway where Don was hanging an ornament from a small gold hook. When they'd first emerged from the attic, he'd shared his suspicions with her that Lilly or Landon had been behind the smoke bomb, then he'd gone straight to the parlor to confront the kids. But everyone must have retired for the night. She'd convinced him to wait until morning. She could see how raw his emotions were and figured waiting until their emotions cooled so the confrontation didn't turn hostile was probably the best path to take. He'd reluctantly agreed. Secretly, she was glad to have some time to get her own emotions in order, especially when they came to him.

There had been such pain in his voice as he talked of his mother's death and his father's desertion. His tale of how the war in the Middle East had left him with the scars of PTSD had hurt her heart. She'd been driven by the need to offer comfort, but the attraction she'd been fighting since the day she'd first laid eyes on him over a year ago had pushed her over the starting line. She'd raced headlong into impulsivity. One chaste kiss on his chin hadn't been enough. She'd practically thrown herself at him by boldly drawing his mouth to hers.

At least he'd had the good sense to raise the checkered flag and end the kiss. Oh, but she'd enjoyed kissing him.

Getting involved with her bodyguard would be a big mistake and she'd end up hurt and alone come New Year's if she did something so impulsive again. He was a by-the-book kind of guy and she…well, she tended to make up the rules as she went.

With resolve to not give in to her feelings, she turned her attention to wrapping the banister in some fake evergreen garland.

"Here," Don said, handing her an ornament. "We can hang these from the greenery.

She took the ornament, pleased by his suggestion. "Good idea."

His gaze searched her face. "Caroline—"

Afraid he wanted to discuss the kiss, she said quickly, "Would you mind hanging the jingle-bell wreath on the front door?"

His mouth quirked, making it clear he knew what she was doing. "Sure."

When they were done, she was pleased with their effort. The house needed some festivity to chase away the gloomy atmosphere pervading the place. "I hope the family will like it."

Don slipped his arm around her waist. "How could they not? You did a great job."

"*We* did a great job." For a moment she was tempted to melt into his arms. But doing so wouldn't lead anywhere either of them wanted to go. Instead, she walked away to push the empty boxes out of the way and into the corner.

Don snagged her hand. "We can take care of those in the morning. You need to sleep."

She allowed him to tug her toward the stairs. Fatigue made lifting one foot in front of the other difficult. She missed a step and would have fallen face-first into the stairs, but Don's strong arms slid around her, steadying her. With a firm grip, he propelled her to her room and pushed the door open. He stepped in and used the flashlight's beam to make sure the room was secure. She appreciated his thoroughness.

"I'm across the hall if you need anything."

"I know, Don. That's why I hired you." She slipped into the room and closed the door firmly behind her and locked it.

She only hoped she could close the door on the memories of their kiss just as easily.

A rustling sound from the far corner of the bedroom raised the fine hairs on Caroline's nape. She lay still, not even remotely sleepy. The storm had quieted down outside. The noise disturbing the silence of her bedroom was definitely coming from inside the dark room. She bolted upright and clutched the fluffy comforter closer.

An inky shadow passed in front of the window. She froze.

Her breath hitched. Her heart stalled out.

Someone was in her room.

Adrenaline spiked, sending her senses careening. She shoved the covers aside and scrambled across the bed. A hand closed over her ankle. A scream burst from her lungs. Terrified, she twisted so she could strike out with her free foot.

Her first attempt missed. Her attacker dragged her closer. She bucked and kicked out again. Her arms flaying as she bent forward and pounded her fists against the hard muscled arms trying to subdue her. A hand yanked a handful of her hair, snapping her head back in a painful burst. Tight fingers groped for her throat and squeezed, cutting off her air supply.

Fresh panic galvanized her. She fought with the fury of survival. Her heel connected with a well-landed shot to the abdomen, eliciting a painful groan. The steel bands gripping her weakened. Taking advantage, she jerked out of her attacker's grasp and crawled off the opposite edge of the bed onto the floor. With another scream she bolted for the door, praying she'd make it.

A piercing scream jackknifed through Don. He'd dozed off, needing to recharge. Now wide awake, he rolled off the bed, snagging the flashlight as he went. He flicked on the beam of light and with his right hand grabbed his Glock from between the mattress and box spring. His legs propelled him forward just as the bedroom door burst open. Caroline launched herself at him.

She trembled against him. "Someone's in my room! He tried to strangle me."

Alarm ripped along Don's nerve endings. He put her behind him and hurried across the hall, leading with his gun, and the flashlight illuminating the way. He swept the beam of light around Caroline's room. Empty. Just as it had been earlier.

Frustration pounded at his temple. He jammed his sidearm into the waistband of his sweat pants and pulled his shirt over it. Whoever had been in her room had escaped. Family member? Or a stranger? If the latter, how had they entered the house? He needed to contact the authorities, get an investigation team here and find the culprit.

"What's happening?" Abigail said as she came down the hall with a candle held in her hand. The flowing robe she wore swirled as she came to a stop.

"We heard you scream," Samuel added, stepping up behind his wife. He'd changed into plaid pj's.

From the opposite direction the twins ran down the hall, the beams of light from their flashlights bouncing as they came. Landon's T-shirt had a silkscreen on the front from a recent teen movie. Lilly wore black baggie sweats that made her impish face seem more pasty white than olive in the dim light.

A door farther down the hall that led to the upstairs rooms adjacent to the attic banged open. Mary, clutching the front of her terry robe, and Horace, still dressed in his dark suit, joined them.

"Sir, is everything all right?" Horace asked.

"There was someone in my room," Caroline said, fisting the back of Don's shirt.

Abigail gasped. "An intruder?"

"I couldn't see who it was. He tried to strangle me." She pushed back the collar of her shirt to show the marks left by the intruder.

Don hated how shaky Caroline's voice sounded. "Whoever it was could still be in the house."

The frantic ring of a bell filled the hall.

"Elijah!" Caroline whirled and raced toward his room. Alarmed by Caroline's lack of regard for her own safety, Don chased after her. The family followed quickly behind.

Elijah's bell quieted as they shoved their way into the room. A hurricane lamp glowed beside the bed revealing his panicked state.

"What's going on? I heard someone scream," Elijah said.

Abigail pushed past Caroline to take Elijah's hand. "Caroline had a scare. Most likely a nightmare. Nothing for you to get upset about."

Suspicion reared. Why would she downplay the attack? To protect Elijah or because she was involved?

"It wasn't a nightmare," Caroline said, pulling aside her robe again to show the bruises forming on her neck. "Someone was there. They must have escaped when I ran into Don's room."

Don concluded the same thing. If he thought she'd be safe with these people he'd go make a sweep of the place, but he wasn't leaving Caroline's side. He groped for a cell phone that wasn't there. "We need to contact the police.

"No one was hurt," Samuel said hastily. "Surely we don't need to drag the sheriff out at this hour. Tomorrow will be soon enough to inform the authorities."

Don narrowed his gaze on Samuel. Why would the man want to keep this quiet? Unless…was he the attacker? Or did he know who it was? If the attacker didn't live in the house, he'd have needed someone to let him in. Rather than outright confronting him, Don challenged, "If the intruder is still in the house the whole family is in danger, right?"

Fear flared in Samuel's face. Was he afraid for his family's safety or afraid his accomplice would be found?

Horace cleared his throat. "I'll contact Sheriff Gantz."

Don's whipped his attention to the butler. "How?"

With a quick glance toward Elijah, who gave an approving nod, Horace said, "I have satellite phone in my quarters."

Anger stirred in Don's gut. Horace and Samuel had held out on him. Was the whole household in cahoots?

With a huff, Samuel headed toward the door. "I'll check all the doors and windows and look for signs of anyone hiding in the house."

"Can I come, too?" Landon asked. The expression on his young face showed his eagerness for adventure.

Samuel hesitated, what appeared to be concern flashing in his eyes, and then he relented. "Come along."

Grinning, Landon followed Samuel out. Lilly started to leave behind the men.

"Lilly, can you please bring your grandfather some fresh water?" Abigail called.

"I can get it, Mrs. Maddox," Mary said, stepping forward to take the empty water goblet from the bedside table.

"Very well," Abigail said. She left Elijah's side to usher her daughter out of the room. "Come along, Lilly."

Once they were alone with Elijah, Caroline hurried to his side. "I'm so sorry to have frightened you."

"Nonsense, child. You're the one who had the scare. I fear this house may not be safe for you."

"He may be right," Don said, glad the old man had brought it up. He couldn't wait to get Caroline out of this den of vipers. "Maybe we could find a hotel." He knew better than to suggest they leave Mississippi altogether. Would she accept this compromise?

"No. I can't. Not until I know for sure no one here is in danger."

Don knew that tone in her voice. It was the same one she'd used when she'd informed him she was coming to Mississippi with or without him. Don blew out a breath. Once Caroline made up her mind, he doubted much would change it. Though he admired her determination and feisty spirit, she wasn't making his job of protecting her any easier.

"I couldn't bear if something happened to you," Elijah said. His gaze sought Don. "There are secret passageways in this house. You need to find them."

Surprise rooted Don to the floor. "I will."

Mary returned with a full glass of water. "Drink some of this, Mr. Maddox."

Don and Caroline moved aside for Mary to help Elijah with the water and straw. When he'd had his fill, he lay back and closed his eyes.

"I'll stay with him," Mary told them as she eased herself into a chair.

They bade Elijah good-night. Don urged Caroline out of the room.

When they were alone, she said, "Secret passages? This house just keeps getting weirder."

"Let's check your room."

Inside her bedroom with the door firmly closed, Don

said, "You take that side of the room and check the walls. If there's a passageway it should sound hollow."

With flashlight in hand, Don moved to the wall and rapped his knuckles against the wood. For several moments, quiet tapping filled the room. Finally they met in the middle of the back wall at the wardrobe. Using his shoulder, Don pushed at the large piece of furniture. It wouldn't budge. He dropped down and shined the flashlight on the wardrobe's feet. They were bolted to the floor. Frustration tightened the muscles of Don's neck. "Nothing."

He straightened and opened the wardrobe doors. "This is big enough for someone to hide in."

"That's creepy," Caroline stated with an edge to her voice.

"Yeah, it is." He inspected the back panel. Flimsy wood, but firmly in place as far as he could tell.

A knock sounded on the door. Don crossed the room and pulled the door open. Horace stood there, his dispassionate expression the same as when he'd opened the door upon their arrival.

"The sheriff is downstairs," Horace said.

"Good. Thank you, Horace." Don motioned for Caroline to follow him. They descended the stairs to find a tall, lanky uniformed man with a thick mustache talking with Samuel and Abigail. The twins stood nearby, inspecting the nativity scene on the oak table.

"Sheriff George Gantz, my niece Caroline Tully and her fiancé, Don Cavanaugh," Samuel said as Don and Caroline joined them.

"I understand someone attacked you, Ms. Tully?" Sheriff Gantz questioned.

"Yes, sir." She went into detail about the attack.

"I searched the house and couldn't find any evidence of a break-in," Samuel said.

Don took Caroline's hand. She jerked in surprise but didn't pull away. Hopefully she'd forgiven him for his unprofessional behavior earlier. Kissing her wasn't part of the job.

But getting to the bottom of who'd locked them in the attic and set the smoke bomb was. He leveled a look at Landon and Lilly. "So were those homemade smoke bombs or leftovers from July?"

The boy flushed a crimson color. "I don't know what you're talking about."

Lilly merely raised an eyebrow.

"What's this about smoke bombs?" asked Samuel.

"Someone locked us in the attic earlier before Caroline was attacked and set off a very colorful display of smoke," Don replied.

Samuel scowled and turned his attention to his children. "Landon, Lilly. Do you know anything about this?"

Lilly snorted. "No. We didn't do anything."

Landon kept his gaze averted from his father and Don. The boy couldn't have looked guiltier if the word was emblazoned across his forehead. But Don doubted the kid had acted alone. No doubt his sister had instigated the prank. She was the one who'd seen them go into the attic.

"Of course you didn't," Abigail said. She waved a bejeweled hand. "It had to have been the intruder Caroline says was in her room."

Beside him, Caroline stiffened. He squeezed her hand.

The smoke had been a childish prank. He could deal

with that. And he would when he had a moment alone with the kid. The intruder was another story. Samuel and Horace had reported no visible signs of a break-in when they'd returned from inspecting the house. Don wasn't sure he bought their assessment, but he wasn't going to leave Caroline's side to do his own inspection. He needed to find a moment alone with the sheriff.

"Elijah said there are secret passageways in the house," Don said, his alert gaze taking in the family's reaction.

Lilly and Landon glanced at each other and snickered. Abigail sighed and Samuel gave a rueful chuckle.

The sheriff's gaze sharpened. "Passages?"

"I'm sorry to say that is untrue," Samuel said. "My father used to tell Isabella and me that tale when we were kids. Believe me, we searched this house from top to bottom and never found any hidden tunnels or passageways. It's a tall tale."

Don should feel relief to know there was no basis of truth in Elijah's claim, yet wary unease lingered. He didn't trust Samuel. Don looked around at the low ceiling in the parlor and remembered the gabled attic and narrow staircase up. A lot of secrets could be hidden with that sort of architecture.

"There doesn't seem to be any danger at the moment," the sheriff said. "But to be safe, I'll have a deputy swing by again in the morning to check on you all."

"Thank you, George, I appreciate you coming out here on Christmas Eve." Samuel shook the sheriff's hand.

"Glad no harm was done," Gantz said with a glance

toward Caroline. "I would suggest you all make a habit of locking your doors."

Her lips pursed but she didn't answer.

"I'll walk you out, Sheriff," Don said, tugging Caroline out the door with him.

Once they were outside and away from the family, Don said, "Sheriff, I'd like to show you something."

Don led Sheriff Gantz to the destroyed tree trunk. Shining his flashlight's beam, he gestured to the burned crack in the middle of the massive live oak. Don watched to see what Gantz's take would be. Shadows obscured the angles of the sheriff's face but not the hike of his eyebrows as he studied the damage.

Caroline gave Don a quizzical look. He was glad for her patience and silence as the sheriff inspected the body of the trunk.

Gantz rubbed his chin. "It looks like this oak was deliberately felled. Those bits and pieces of metal aren't from lightning."

Bingo. Don was glad to know the sheriff was sharp and observant. "I'm thinking a low-grade IED. Not as sophisticated as some I've seen, but it got the job done."

"Just like my door," Caroline interjected.

Sheriff Gantz's gaze swung to Caroline. "Door?"

Don explained about the bomb at Caroline's apartment. "The Boston Police Department said if the device had been facing up instead of down, Caroline would have died from the blast."

"You didn't tell me that," Caroline said in a hushed voice.

He hadn't seen the point in scaring her with the detail. "Whoever set up your explosive was an amateur." Don pointed to the trunk of the tree. "This one was a better attempt."

"Why blow up the tree?" Caroline asked.

Don exchanged a look with the sheriff.

"As a distraction," Don stated.

"For your attacker to enter the house unseen. All it would take is one unobserved moment to sneak in and hide," finished the sheriff. "No wonder there weren't any signs of forced entry. The unidentified suspect was too good to leave any evidence behind."

SIX

A shudder ripped through Caroline. Don slipped his arm around her. She'd endured a great deal this past week. More than most people could bear. But he'd be here for her if it became too much.

"Another thing. When we were driving here from the airport, a dark green Chevy S-10 pickup tried to force us into a head-on collision," Don informed Gantz.

"You get a license plate?"

Don shook his head. "Plates had been removed."

"Sheriff, do you know Dr. Reese?" Caroline asked.

Gantz nodded. "Yes, ma'am. He's as fine a doctor as they come. Why do you ask?"

"You are aware that Mr. Elijah Maddox is ill?" Don asked.

"I'd heard as much. But I understand it isn't a life-threatening disease."

"It shouldn't be, but Mr. Maddox isn't getting better."

"He's convinced someone is trying to kill him," Caroline said.

"Does he have any proof?" Gantz's tone was sharp.

"No," Don answered. "We intend to talk to Dr. Reese as soon as possible."

"As will I," Gantz promised. "In the meantime, if you have any more trouble, you have Horace give my office a call. I don't live too far from here. I'll have the electric company out here first thing in the morning to repair the downed electrical wires and have my crime-scene techs gather what they can from the tree. However with the rain, any evidence will most likely be washed away."

"Thank you, Sheriff." Don shook his hand.

Worry churned in Don's gut as he and Caroline made their way back inside the house. He couldn't leave her in her room alone and they couldn't stay the remainder of the night, or morning as the case may be, in the same room, either. There had to be somewhere safe in the house. Someplace she could rest without fear.

"Come on." He guided her up the stairs and down the hall to Lilly's door. He knocked softly.

"Don? What are you doing?" Caroline tugged to free her hand.

He held on. "I saw bunk beds in her room."

A moment later, the teenager cracked open the door. Half of her face was visible in the beam of the flashlight. "What?"

Ignoring the surly tone, Don said, "Your cousin needs to stay with you for the rest of the night."

Lilly frowned. "No, she doesn't."

"Yes, she does," Don insisted, not about to let this girl deny Caroline entry. He gestured to Caroline's neck where the marks were still visible. Knowing she'd been hurt twisted his gut into knots. "We need your help, Lilly."

The kid's gaze darted to Caroline, drifting down to Caroline's neck where her delicate skin was marred with light bruises, and back to Don. She rolled her eyes but stepped back and opened the door wider.

"This is not a good idea," Caroline whispered to Don.

"You have a better one?" he whispered back.

She shook her head. Then she crossed the threshold into the teen's domain. "Thank you, Lilly. I appreciate it."

Lilly grunted her acceptance of the thank-you.

Don shut the door behind Caroline. He hoped he wasn't making a mistake. But to be on the safe side, he grabbed a pillow and blanket from his room and made a makeshift bedroll outside Lilly's bedroom door. No one was getting in or out, without him knowing.

Holding her candle up, Caroline used the glow to examine Lilly's room. The pink walls notwithstanding, the covers on the bunk beds were also pink. The dresser was painted pink. A pink fuzzy chair butted up against a white vanity with pink flowers decorating the edge of the mirror. It was like stepping into a ball of cotton candy.

"You like pink," Caroline commented.

Lilly climbed into the bottom bunk and blew out the candle on the table beside her. "I detest pink."

"Then why is your room so pink?"

"Mom's doing. It's been this way since I was kid." She rolled over, presenting Caroline with her back. "G'night."

Shaking her head at the teen's rudeness, Caroline climbed up the ladder to the top bunk and blew out her candle. Not sure what to do with the holder now, she settled on placing the unlit candle on the corner of the mattress against the wall. She burrowed under the pink cover.

Lord, please keep me safe. Keep us all safe.

She prayed like she hadn't in two years. With fervor and heartfelt pleas. She silently recited scriptures, needing the comfort and assurance from God's word like she never had before.

God is my rock, my refuge and my ever-present help in trouble.

She *was* in trouble. Someone wanted her dead. And the only thing standing between her and an assassin was Don.

Muted daylight awoke Caroline. She was still tired from so few hours of sleep. She shifted on the narrow bunk bed, her back aching from the limited space. She missed the comfortable mattress she'd started the night on in her designated room. Remembering the attack, the grip of fingers digging into her neck, sent a shudder coursing through her. At least she'd made it through her first night in the Maddox house alive.

She slipped from the top bunk, her bare feet landing on the pink shag rug. The floorboard creaked beneath her. She sent a quick glance at the huddled figure on the lower bunk. Lilly still slept. The girl's dark hair fanned over the pillow and covered her face, she curled in the fetal position, her hands fisted in the pink covers. Tenderness filled Caroline. No matter how irritating or rude Lilly was, she was still a child.

The yearning for children of her own hit Caroline with the force of a physical blow. She and Cullen had talked about having several because Caroline wanted her children to have siblings. Growing up an only child had at times been lonely and had added to her sense of displacement.

Caroline wanted a big family, a loving home. A place where there was no question she belonged.

Now she despaired she'd never have that. Doubted she'd ever allow herself to hope again. To trust her heart fully to another man again. Shaking off her melancholy thoughts, she opened the bedroom door and barely stopped herself in time to keep from tripping over Don. He was stretched out on his back across the threshold, his head resting on a pillow, a blanket covering his torso. His eyes were closed.

Her heart melted. He took his job seriously. But did he care for her? Did she want him to?

Over the past year, she'd often thought of Don, remembering his kindness, his handsomeness, part of her wishing he'd asked her out, but yet thankful he hadn't, because she wasn't sure her demolished heart would ever be free to love again. She bent to touch his T-shirt-clad shoulder.

His eyes popped open. "You okay?"

Affection infused her. His first concern was for her. Not if something external was wrong. She felt special, cared for.

Slow down, girl. He's doing his job.

The thought slapped down the gentle emotions rising to the surface. She was paying him to be concerned about her. And just because he'd kissed her with so much enthusiasm last night didn't mean his feelings went deeper than client-employer. He'd never shown more than polite interest, until last night. And letting herself wish otherwise would only lead to more pain she didn't want to feel.

She pasted a smile on her face. "I'm fine. But you must be hurting. That floor can't be comfortable."

A slow grin spread across his lips. "I've had a worse night's sleep."

During his time in the Middle East, no doubt. Still, he shouldn't have to sleep in the hall. She stood and reached out to help him up. He slid his bigger, callused hand in hers, sending fissures of warmth up her arm, making her yearn for more. How could such an innocent touch stir such need in her?

When he was standing, she withdrew her hand. Immediately she felt bereft of his touch.

He tucked a curl behind her ear. "You sleep okay?"

The light wisp of his finger brushing her skin sent a frisson tumbling through her. She took a step way, needing some distance between them. "Decently. But we have to figure out some other sleeping arrangement. I won't have you sleeping on the floor again."

He arched an eyebrow. "All part of the job."

Indeed. But she still didn't want him to suffer unduly on her account.

Elsewhere in the house, the sound of jingle bells on a door opening and closing reminded her of the significance of the day. "Merry Christmas."

His expression softened. "Merry Christmas."

She stared up into his blue-green eyes. Images of tropical islands and white-sand beaches danced across her mind. Her and Don romping through the surf, hand and hand. A couple. On their honeymoon.

"What are you thinking?" he asked. "You have a very dreamy expression right now."

She blinked, startled out of her musing. Her cheeks flamed, the burning sensation traveling to her very core. She put her hands to her cheeks to cool the heat flushing through her. What was it about Don that made her forget reason? "I need to go to my room."

With a lopsided smile, he gestured with his hand for her to lead the way. Conscious of him close behind her, she hurried to her room and slipped inside. She heard him chuckle as she closed the door. She rested against the portal. What was wrong with her? Her life was being threatened. Her biological grandfather was slowly dying, possibly being murdered. And she was indulging in fantasies starring her *fake* fiancé.

She'd better get a grip on reality. Don wasn't her fiancé. And she had no intention of going down the hazardous path of romance again.

With that thought firmly in place, she went to the window and opened the curtain all the way, allowing gray daylight to spread over the room. Secret passage-ways. Hmm. They'd checked the walls. Where else could there be a secret opening?

She checked the floorboards, pulling up the colorful area rug, but couldn't find a hint of a trap door.

However someone *had* been in her room. She'd heard him, seen his shadow. Felt his fingers around her throat.

A chill of fright prickled her skin.

Despite a locked door and a bodyguard, she'd come close to dying last night. She could only pray God would watch over them all.

Don strapped an ankle holster to the inside of his left leg and jammed his Glock into the slot on the inner side. Pulling his jean leg down, he concealed the weapon. He hoped it wouldn't be needed, but after last night, he had a feeling things were only going to get worse.

He knocked on Caroline's door. No answer. Anxiety kicked up, making his heart race. He opened the door. The room was empty. Had she gone downstairs without him?

Hurrying downstairs, he found the Maddox family, minus Elijah, at the table. He slipped into the seat next to Caroline. Now was not the time to lecture her about not waiting for him to escort her.

She smiled a greeting but a distance in her eyes didn't sit well with him. Concerned, he studied her. Though she'd said she'd slept decently, dark circles appeared beneath her tawny eyes. A knot formed in his chest. Despite how calm and collected she appeared with her hair gathered into a clip at her nape and the scooped collar of her red blouse accentuating the slender column of her throat, tension visibly tightened around her mouth. And he hated to see the marks on her neck from last night's attack—proof that he hadn't been able to protect her well enough. But in spite of everything, she sat straight and tall.

She was trying hard to be brave and strong. Admiration and affection grew, making him want to shield her from the horrors of this world, not just physically but emotionally, like a real fiancé would.

A warning bell went off in his head. *Stop right there, Cavanaugh. You're her bodyguard not her fiancé.* Thinking of them together, as a couple, could get her killed. Stay uninvolved emotionally. Yeah, right. Like he hadn't already broken that rule a hundred times since she'd walked into Trent Associates. *Lame, dude. Really lame.*

"Caroline, I wanted to say thank you for putting out so many decorations. The entryway and parlor are so cheery," Abigail said with a pleased smile.

"You're welcome," Caroline replied. She lifted a glass of orange juice. "Merry Christmas."

"Hear, hear," Samuel said, holding up his glass. "Merry Christmas and welcome to the newly returned member of our family and her fiancé."

Don raised his glass. "Merry Christmas. May we all make it through the next week without mishap."

Caroline met his gaze. "I'll drink to that." She sipped from her glass.

"So when are your nuptials?" Abigail asked over the rim of her cup of coffee.

"Spring—" Caroline said.

"Summer—" Don said at the same time.

Playing the fiancé to the hilt, he stretched his arm around Caroline's shoulders. He told himself the possessive gesture was for show, but he couldn't quite make himself believe it, not when touching her felt so natural, so right. "We haven't finalized the details."

Abigail smiled. "There are lots of details to decide upon. I planned Samuel's and my wedding. I would be happy to help you, Caroline. Would you like a traditional church wedding or something more modern?"

Caroline choked on a sip of juice.

Don patted her back. "You're kind to offer. We'll absolutely consider your generosity."

Feeling Caroline stiffen, he steered the conversation away from his and Caroline's engagement. "Samuel, do you have a car I could borrow? Our rental is still trapped by the fallen tree."

"Of course, you're welcome to use my Bentley. May I ask where you intend to drive?"

"Down the road until I can get a signal on my cell."

Samuel pinned him with a curious look. "Is there something you require?"

"Work. I need to check in with some clients."

"What kind of work do you, Donovan?" Abigail asked.

"Investments," he answered easily because he was telling the truth. He had a personal side business— managing several portfolios for former protectees and for James Trent in addition to his work at Trent Associates.

Numbers had always come easily. After his tour of duty, he'd attended night classes at Woods College of Advancing Studies, a division of Boston College, and achieved a professional studies certificate in finance. Trent had even footed the tuition, claiming they could use a financial person in-house.

Samuel perked up. "Really? I could use some advice on a few stock options that I've been thinking of investing in."

Aware of Caroline's studied gaze, Don said, "I'd love to hear what you're thinking and if I can help, I will."

Beneath the table, Caroline touched his leg. He grasped her hand and gave a gentle squeeze, silently promising to fill her in later.

The rest of the breakfast went by in small talk. When they were done with the eggs Benedict and trays of fresh fruit, the family retired to the parlor while Don escorted Caroline upstairs to visit her grandfather.

"Do you really know stocks and investments?" she whispered as they walked down the hall.

"Yes. It started out more a hobby and became its own side business."

"Impressive. I didn't realize you were a numbers guy as well as a bodyguard."

He refrained from saying she didn't know a lot about him.

They reached the end of the hall and Caroline knocked on Elijah's bedroom door before entering. The old man's eyes were closed. His skin was pale in the dim light coming through the cracks in the drawn curtain. Apprehension twisted Don's gut. Asleep? Or dead?

Caroline checked Elijah's pulse. Her shoulders visibly relaxed. Asleep.

"Let's not disturb him," she whispered, drawing Don from the room. "Are you really checking in with clients?"

"Trent Associates. Though James is technically a client," Don clarified. "Horace is very protective of his satellite phone. Besides, too many ears here."

Understanding danced across Caroline's face.

"I want to have the office run a background check on the doctor. And find out why the New Orleans Police Department left out such an important detail of no forced entry into Isabella's apartment."

She twirled the gold-studded earring in her left ear. He could see her mind working. "I'll stay here."

"No can do. Which reminds me we need to have a talk about you not wandering this house alone."

"But I want to read Isabella's diary and yearbook."

"Bring them with you. I don't want you out of my sight."

She laid her hand on his arm. The pressure gentle, yet searing. "Isn't that going a little overboard?"

He covered her hand with his own, stemming the urge to pull her into his arms and kiss her again, to show her how very important she was becoming to him. He forced words out despite the constriction in his chest. "Not when it comes to your safety."

She blinked, her gaze dipping to where their skin touched. When she raised her gaze, the yearning in her eyes nearly undid his self-control.

Slipping her hand away, she backed up as if she too felt the need to put distance between them before they did something they'd regret. Developing a relationship under tense circumstance wasn't a wise choice for anyone.

"I'll meet you downstairs in ten minutes."

Watching her hurry to her room, Don tried to recite his Rules of Protection but they stuck in his throat.

Okay, Lord, I'm going to need Your strength here. Because obviously when it came to Caroline, the rules went out the window.

The soothing patter of rain pelting the exterior of the car created an insular atmosphere. Caroline snuggled deeper into the butter-soft passenger seat of Samuel's borrowed Bentley. The interior smelled of polished leather. The wood grain inlaid dashboard gleamed. Definitely better maintained than the manor house. "I don't know much about cars, but this one must be worth a pretty penny. Part of the estate, or Samuel's personal property?"

"Good question." Don pulled the car into a turnout and cut the engine. He checked his phone. "Got a signal."

Within a few moments he was connected to Trent Associates and was relaying the events since they'd arrived to someone named Simone. It occurred to Caroline that bodyguards didn't take days off even for holidays. She glanced at Don and tried not to notice the strong line of his jaw or the way the timbre of his voice slid pleasant little shivers down her spine. She liked how dedicated he was.

Despite her best intentions, it was impossible to ignore her growing attraction to and affection for her bodyguard. She was so thankful she wasn't going through this alone. She needed him, his quiet strength and steady presence.

And she found herself wanting more.

More of his touches, more of his kisses.

Thinking about what her life would be like when this was over, when he was no longer her protector, made her ache in ways she vowed she wouldn't allow again. Letting her heart become attached to Don would only lead to heartache because she wasn't sure she could trust her heart to anyone again.

Disgusted with her foolishness, she flipped through Isabella's yearbook, scanning the pictures and the names hoping for a glimpse of her birth mother. She curled the edges of the pages, bookmarking the places where Isabella Maddox's name appeared. She'd been in the chess club, freshman student council, the school newspaper and the debate club.

As she read the names beneath the group photo, a particular name jumped out at her sending her heart pounding.

"I appreciate it, Simone," Don said into the phone. "Thank you."

As soon as he clicked off, Caroline said, "Look at this." She angled the yearbook so Don could see where she was pointing. "Randall Paladin—the lawyer who contacted me about the estate—and my mother were in the same debate club."

Don's jaw tightened. "Now that *is* interesting."

"Can you call him? Set up an appointment?" she asked, anxious to talk to the man. "He knew my mother. Maybe he can shed some light on who she was seeing."

Don punched in the number for information and asked the operator for Paladin's number. Antsy with anticipation, Caroline tapped her foot, the rhythmic sound filling the interior of the car.

Punching End on the cell phone, Don said, "Got a recorded message. The office is closed today but will be open tomorrow."

Trying not to be disappointed, she closed the yearbook. "Then we'll have to wait until then. What did your friend have to say at Trent?"

"Simone will check with N.O.P.D. and get back to me." He held out his phone. "Would you like to call your parents?"

Grateful for his thoughtfulness, she took the phone and punched in her parent's number. When her mother answered, Caroline's heart squeezed tight. It was strange not to be home on Christmas. She could imagine the smells of gingerbread cake and turkey roasting in the oven. Talking to her parents made Caroline homesick. But they were safe and that was what mattered most to her. As she hung up, she sighed.

"Everything all right?" Don asked.

Handing back his phone, she nodded. "Yes. They're good. I miss them. This is my first Christmas away from them."

"You never celebrated with Cullen's family?"

Surprise washed over her. Don's sensitivity was endearing. "No. Cullen's parents divorced when he was young. His dad lives in California and his mother retired to Florida around the time we met. Neither one did much for the holidays. Spending Christmas with my family made Cullen happy."

"I'd imagine spending the time with you was what made him happy."

She met his gaze and liked the kindness in his eyes. And wished his words were true. But in the end, she knew Cullen had preferred someone else's company. "Thank you for saying that."

He shrugged. "I know how I'd feel."

She raised an eyebrow, not sure how to take his comment. But more important, not sure she wanted to delve where the comment could lead. Don was quickly breaching the barricade she'd erected around her heart without even trying. What would happen if he really tried to make her fall for him?

She'd be a goner for sure. So not going to happen.

As if he'd realized how revealing his words were, he flashed a sheepish smile and without another word started the engine. He pulled the Bentley back out onto the road. Charged silence filled the car. When they arrived back at the house two vans were parked out front. Men were working on the power lines while a crew worked to clear the fallen tree from the driveway.

As they entered the house, Samuel came out of the

library. "Ah, you're back. Don, do you have a few moments to talk about my portfolio?"

Caroline could see his hesitation. His words about her not wandering through the house alone echoed in her head. But she needed a couple minutes of solitude. "Go. I'd like to take a short nap anyway."

"I'll walk you up."

"No need."

She could tell he wanted to argue, but with Samuel watching he refrained. "Yell if you need me."

Though his tone was light, there was caution lacing the words. He meant *scream.* "I will."

For Samuel's sake, she leaned close, intending to brush a kiss against his cheek like a loving fiancé would. He turned his head and their lips met. A sweet, gentle kiss that she wanted to linger in. Samuel's chuckle jerked her back to reality. They were pretending to be engaged. But that didn't feel like pretend. Just as the kiss the night before hadn't felt fake.

And one look in Don's eyes made her believe he felt the same buzz of attraction. Didn't he realize there was nothing but disaster there?

SEVEN

Caroline hurried up the stairs. Lilly and Landon emerged from a room to her right. The pesky pair blocked her way.

Caroline crossed her arms like her favorite English teacher and asked, "Hey, guys, what's up?"

Her gaze shifted between the two teens. Their dark expressions sent a chill tripping down her back. Where was their Christmas spirit and goodwill?

"You need to leave," Lilly demanded, her voice edged in anger.

Okay, the kid had nothing on Scrooge. Caroline arched an eyebrow, not liking the girl's attitude.

"We don't want you here," Landon added. "You're an outsider."

Not sure how to respond to such blatant hostility, Caroline sought to diffuse the situation. They were kids, she reminded herself, not monsters. At least she prayed so.

"I realize this is a difficult time right now. With your grandfather sick and strangers in the house—"

"You just want his money," Lilly sneered. "But

you're not entitled to it. You haven't lived here, taking care of Grandfather the way we have."

Was the kid reiterating words she'd heard from her father and mother? "You're right, I haven't been here. I didn't know about any of you."

"Well, now you do. And we don't want you here," Lilly said.

Landon turned on his sister. "That's what I said."

Lilly shot him a glare. "Shut up."

"Make me," Landon taunted.

Lilly rolled her eyes and then pointed a finger at Caroline. "You don't belong here."

"So you've said," Caroline replied, her patience wearing thin.

"Lilly! Landon!" Abigail glided toward them. "What are you doing?"

"Nothing," Landon muttered.

Lilly's mouth scrunched up in a sullen pout.

"Leave your cousin alone," Abigail said. She gave Caroline an apologetic smile. "Never mind them, dear. We don't have many visitors."

As if such a flimsy excuse would explain the teens' rudeness. "No worries, Abigail. I don't scare easily."

Abigail flared her nostrils and squared her shoulders. "I am quite certain if the children's intent had been to scare you, Caroline, your hair would be standing on end."

Outrage had Caroline tucking back her chin. "Excuse me?"

With a sigh, Abigail visibly reined in her displeasure. "They've run off several tutors over the years."

"Ah. I see." But was the twin's naughtiness of a malicious nature? Just how far would they go? The question lingered in Caroline's mind as Abigail hustled the kids away.

Contrary to her words, Caroline was shaken by her encounter with her cousins.

Apprehension rippled over her as she thought how vulnerable she'd been snoozing away on the top bunk in Lilly's room. With so much anger simmering beneath the surface, would the girl harm Caroline during the night if she once again slept in the bunk bed?

Had one of them been in her room last night?

No, whoever had attacked her had been big and muscular.

One thing was certain—Caroline would not be sleeping in the teen's room again.

She retreated to the original bedroom she'd been assigned and trying to think like Don, she pulled the ladder-back chair from the front of the vanity table to the door. She tilted the chair back and wedged it beneath the engraved brass door handle, then turned the lock.

She turned to stare at the wardrobe. Glancing around, her gaze landed on the brass table lamp. Quickly she unplugged the lamp and then, wielding it like a weapon, approached the wardrobe. Gathering her courage, she yanked open the doors, prepared to bash an intruder on the head. The wardrobe was empty.

A relieved and embarrassed laugh bubbled. She closed the doors and replaced the lamp. Feeling relatively safe, she curled up on the bed with Isabella's diary and college yearbook.

She opened the diary. The words flowed in neatly penned script. Isabella wrote of her excitement to be going off to college, her classes and things she was learning. About halfway through the journal, she mentioned two men, one of whom she loved and the other she wished would leave her alone. But oddly and to Caroline's complete frustration only once did she mention a name—Johnny.

Could this be Caroline's father or the name of Isabella's stalker? Despite her aggravation at the lack of straightforward answers, Caroline couldn't help but be moved by the description of the man Isabella loved.

> *He makes me feel so special and cared for. He doesn't put unrealistic expectations on me but accepts me, as I am, flaws and all. He's seen me at my worst and at my best.*

The words resonated within Caroline. She knew a man who made her feel exactly the same way. She closed her eyes, letting her mind bring up his image; only it was Don's face she saw in her mind, not Cullen's. She shook her head, trying to dispel the image, but it wouldn't go away. Her eyelids popped open. Dismay flooded her.

Oh, no. No, no, no. She couldn't allow herself to fall for Don. It didn't matter how Don made her pulse race or the joy spending time with him gave her. Allowing herself to be vulnerable to love again was a risk she wouldn't take.

Focusing back on the diary, she pushed her disturbing emotions and thoughts aside and continued to read. Tears misted her eyes as she read Isabella's words of love for the baby growing inside her. And her fear of what would become of both of them.

Why didn't she write of marrying the man whose

child she carried? Where was this man she loved? Why wasn't he there for Isabella?

Caroline's heart broke for her young mother.

The entries skipped ahead by several months. Fear constricted Caroline's throat as the words jumped off the page.

> *He's outside my apartment again. I don't want his attention, but I don't know how to get through to him. My heart belongs to another. But he won't accept that. I worry what he'll do when he learns about the baby.*

Caroline's stomach twisted. Isabella had been more afraid of this man than she was of being an unwed mother. Had this man found out that Isabella carried another man's child and become so enraged that he killed her?

The last entry was dated the day of Caroline's birth.

> *My water broke this morning. I'm heading to the hospital. I should be excited and happy, but my heart grieves for what I have to do, but it's for the best. For all of us. The social worker says a very nice couple is waiting for my little girl. I pray they will love her as much as I do.*

A sob echoed in the quiet room. Caroline hadn't realized she was crying. She wiped at the tears flowing down her cheeks.

Whether he was Isabella's lover or stalker, Caroline knew that this man named Johnny was the key to her mother's past.

She needed to ask the family about Johnny. She hurried downstairs to start with her uncle.

As she entered the library Don and Samuel looked up. A ledger was open on the desk.

Irritation flashed in Samuel's eyes before a welcoming smile crossed his lips. "Caroline, your young man knows his stuff."

Caroline didn't regret interrupting. She had questions for her uncle.

Don regarded her with concern. "Is everything okay?"

No doubt her eyes were red from crying. She gave him a reassuring smile. "I'm fine. I need to ask Samuel something." She addressed the older man. "Did you and my mother know someone named Johnny?"

He cocked his head. "Why do you ask?"

Was that recognition in his gaze? "Isabella mentions a Johnny in her diary. I was wondering if she was dating a man by that name."

"I see." He closed the ledger and put it in the top desk drawer. "Can't say that I recall any Johnny in Isabella's life."

"Did you know she was being harassed by a man before I was born?"

Samuel's eyes widened. "What do you mean, harassed?"

"She wrote about a man who wouldn't leave her alone. Who wouldn't accept she was in love with someone else. Do you know who my mother was afraid of?"

Don came to her side. His support was so very needed.

Samuel shook his head. "I don't have the foggiest."

"Maybe Elijah will know," Don suggested.

"I would prefer you didn't upset my father," Samuel stated coming around the desk. "The subject of Isabella is very painful for us all. There's no sense in dredging up the past now."

Don's gaze narrowed, and Caroline knew they were both thinking the same thing. Dredging up Isabella's past might be the only way to catch a killer.

The following morning, Don and Caroline drove to town with a full agenda. First, a stop at Elijah's doctor's office, then a visit to Randall Paladin, Esquire. This time they took the rental sedan since Samuel had left earlier for his office in the Bentley.

"I've been meaning to ask, what were your thoughts on Samuel's portfolio?" Caroline sat in the passenger seat, lightly tapping her short, neat nails on the door handle.

"He's an aggressive investor and has several nice annuities coming in from various funds." Don had been impressed by Samuel's meticulous record-keeping.

"So he has his own money apart from Elijah?"

"He does. Plus a salary for managing all of the Maddox family properties."

She raised her eyebrows. "Are there many?"

"Elijah holds the deeds on most of the buildings downtown and several homes in Jefferson County. Worth a few million."

"So there is something to inherit," Caroline stated with a frown. "But with all those assets, why has the Maddox house been so neglected?"

"Seems odd to me, too. Especially with how detail-oriented Samuel appears to be. Hopefully Mr. Paladin can shed some light on the issue. Maybe there are legalities we're not aware of."

Caroline nodded and turned her attention forward as they drove down Fayette's main drag. "This is such a lovely, quaint place."

The town square was decked out with garlands and red bows. Brick buildings painted in bright colors stacked side by side made for interesting visuals. Don parked the car in an angled slot near the Fayette Health Clinic's front door.

He climbed out of the vehicle and went around the front to open the passenger door for Caroline. A prickling sensation at the base of his skull, an unheard whisper of danger, sent his senses into hyperalert mode.

Too often he'd skirted to close to death not to pay attention to the internal warning that could only come from God. And each time he could look back and see the divine way God had moved to protect him.

He'd stumbled at the exact moment a sniper's bullet zoomed a hairsbreadth from his head. When his transport had run out of gas, even though they'd just filled the tank, he and his company had climbed out seconds before a IED exploded, demolishing the vehicle.

And he'd felt this exact prickling sensation at the base of his skull warning of danger when he'd walked into an ambush, which had allowed him to neutralize the threat, saving his life and the lives of his team.

The imprinted memories of those times shuddered through him. He rubbed the back of his neck trying to erase the lingering terror of war.

He didn't doubt God's existence or His presence. Don just didn't get why some prayers were answered and others weren't.

Placing a protective arm around Caroline's waist, his body prepared to move at any sign of danger. He searched the street, the sidewalks and the surrounding buildings, looking for a threat. No one seemed to be paying any attention to them. But still the impression persisted.

"Don?"

"We're being watched," he said.

Caroline melded closer, a flash of fear pinching the corners of her eyes. "Who? Where?"

He shook his head. He couldn't see anything, but his certainty wasn't shaken.

"Let's go." Don hurried her to the glass double doors beneath a red awning. As soon as they were safely inside, he glanced back toward the street. Someone was out there, watching, waiting. It would be only a matter of time before Caroline's unknown attacker struck again.

Don would be ready.

The doctor's office waiting room was packed with several children and their concerned parents. A pregnant woman looking decidedly uncomfortable sat near the door and an older couple clung to each other in the corner.

Don ushered Caroline to the front desk.

"We'd like to speak with Dr. Reese," Don said when the receptionist looked their way. She was older with glasses and a harried expression.

"Do you have an appointment?" Her tone suggested they'd better, or else.

"No, we don't," Caroline spoke up. "I'm Elijah Maddox's granddaughter. I have a question about his care."

The receptionist's eyebrows shot up. "I'll see if he'll have time to talk to you. Please have a seat."

They took seats near the far wall. Caroline leaned over to whisper, "Did you see the way she reacted when I mentioned Elijah's name?"

Don nodded. The Maddox name obviously had some pull.

A few minutes passed before a smiling young woman stepped out. She had a stethoscope around her neck. "Ms. Maddox?"

Caroline rose.

"Follow me, please."

They were ushered to an office. Framed degrees hung on the wall. A window overlooking Main Street allowed in natural light. Two armchairs faced a clutter-free desk.

"Dr. Reese will be with you in a moment."

The nurse exited, shutting the door behind her. Caroline sat in one of the chairs. Don moved to the window and leaned against the sill.

A moment later the door opened and an older gentleman entered. His full head of salt-and-pepper hair was parted down the middle. A Roman nose and long jaw gave his face character.

He stuck out his hand. "Ms. Maddox, I'm Dr. Gerry Reese. Elijah had mentioned he'd found his long-lost grandchild."

Caroline shook his hand. "Caroline Tully."

"I'm sure Elijah must be overjoyed to finally have you in his life." Reese turned his attention to Don. "And you are?"

Don straightened and held out his hand. "Donovan Cavanaugh, Caroline's fiancé."

Reese's smile widened. "Excellent. What can I do for you two this morning?"

"We'd like to ask you about Elijah's illness," Don said, gauging the man's reaction.

Reese frowned as he rounded his desk and leaned against the side. "He hasn't taken another turn for the worse has he?"

"No but he doesn't seem to be improving," Don answered, watching the doctor closely. "How long have you been Elijah's doctor?"

"You understand that because of HIPPA laws I can't discuss his medical care with you."

Don did understand and appreciated the man's ethics. He pulled out a folded note written by Elijah giving the doctor permission to talk to them.

He handed the note over. "We're not asking you to break doctor-patient confidentiality."

"We just want to know how to make him better," Caroline interjected.

Don liked the way they were in tune with each other's thoughts.

Reese stared into her eyes, taking her measure. The doctor shook his head. "To tell you the truth, I don't understand Elijah's struggle with Addison's. His disease isn't life threatening and the medications I've prescribed should be managing it. People with Addison's can live normal lives. I should do some more testing. Could you bring him in later this week?"

"I'm sure we can arrange something," Don said.

"Good." Reese pushed away from the desk. "I'm sorry to cut this short but I have patients waiting."

Once they were out on the sidewalk, Caroline asked, "What did you think of him?"

Keeping a vigilant eye out for any signs of danger, he positioned himself to act as her shield as they moved along the sidewalk. "He seems to be a competent physician. But to be on the safe side, I think we should arrange for a second opinion."

"Me, too." A pensive look crossed her features. "Do you think maybe someone is poisoning Elijah?"

"The thought has crossed my mind. Maybe in his food."

If so, he needed to find out who and how before Caroline became the next victim. The very idea of anything happening to her made his gut clench and his heart race. He'd gone way beyond breaking the rules.

He was starting to care deeply for his fake fiancé.

"Do you think Mary is the one...?" Caroline winced as her words trailed off. "She seems like such a sweet woman. Why?"

Don had the same thought. "Maybe Samuel's paying her?"

"You really believe he's behind everything, don't you?"

"I do."

"I'm going to start preparing his meals," Caroline stated with a determined note in her voice.

Admiring how her sharp mind worked, Don cautioned, "Might be hard to justify something like that without explanation."

She deflated. "True.

"Tell Mary you'd like to learn some of her recipes."

The spark was back. "Good idea."

Her pleased smile smacked into him like a punch to the solar plexus. He forced his gaze away. "Let's find Paladin's office."

The law firm was on the second floor of a redbrick building with a green awning. They took the stairs and entered the plush reception area. A blonde sat at a desk talking on the phone. She held up a hand acknowledging their presence.

When she hung up, she smiled. "How can I help you?"

Don gestured to Caroline. "This is Caroline Tully, Elijah Maddox's granddaughter."

Her eyes widened. "Just a moment." She rose and walked down the hall to knock on a closed door. A muffled voice bade her enter. She disappeared inside for a moment, then returned.

"Mr. Paladin will see you. Right this way," she motioned toward the room she'd left.

Don placed his hand at the small of Caroline's back and followed her into Paladin's office. Playing the protective fiancé in public wasn't a hardship. But remembering that it was only pretend was proving more difficult all the time.

The expansive office was handsomely decorated. Framed degrees and certificates graced the wall behind the well-dressed man sitting at the L-shaped mahogany desk. A credenza sat off to the side with neatly stacked file folders, thick law books and several small framed family photos.

Paladin rose and came around the front of the desk to offer Caroline his hand. He had a full head of salted hair that once might have been very blond. Don guessed him to be in his early fifties.

"Ms. Tully, I hope your stay in Mississippi has been pleasant."

Giving his hand a quick shake, she muttered, "Not really."

Don hid a smile. Caroline wasn't one to hedge.

A crease formed on the older man's brow. "I'm troubled to hear that. Is there anything I can do to assist you?"

"We have some questions," she replied.

Paladin's gray eyes shot to Don. "You must be Caroline's fiancé."

Don gripped the older man's hand. He had a firm handshake, smooth skin and manicured nails. "Donovan Cavanaugh."

Paladin returned to his seat and waved a hand toward the two chairs facing the desk. "Please, have a seat. Tell me how I can help?"

"How long have you been Elijah's lawyer?" Don asked.

"I took over my father's practice nearly fifteen years ago," he answered, his voice silky like a politician's. "My father and Mr. Maddox go back to their childhood."

"You grew up here," Caroline said.

"I did indeed."

Wanting to get to the heart of why they were there, Don asked, "Did you know Isabella Maddox?"

Paladin sat back in his chair and regarded him with a steady gaze. "Since we were children. You know we both went to the same university, Tulane?"

"I do. You were in the debate club together," Caroline said.

Surprise flashed in the older man's eyes. "That is correct. How did you…?"

"I found my mother's freshman yearbook."

"Ah, yes. Your mother was a lovely woman." His eyes narrowed slightly. "Your resemblance to her is quite uncanny."

Don detected an odd note in Paladin's tone but couldn't place his finger on it. "Were you in New Orleans when she was murdered?"

Sadness flickered in the lawyer's eyes. "Yes, I was. I was entering my final year that fall. The whole school was very shaken up by the tragedy."

"Do you know who she was seeing at the time?" Caroline asked.

Paladin's gaze shifted to her. His expression didn't change but Don sensed a distancing in the man.

"Do you mean do I know who your father is?" He shook his head. "Isabella and I didn't keep in close contact. I saw her at debate club and occasionally in the halls or on the quad, but I don't have the slightest idea who she was keeping company with."

Disappointment was written across Caroline's lovely face. Don reached over to take her hand. She held on tight.

"How about a Johnny?" Don asked.

The lawyer blinked. "Do you have a last name?"

Caroline sat forward on the edge of the chair. "No last name. Was there a Johnny in school with my mother?"

"My dear, Tulane is a big school. I'm sure there were many men named John in attendance. If you had a last name you could call the school registrar and have them do a search. But without that…" He made a helpless gesture.

Though Paladin's words made sense, Don couldn't help but think there was something the lawyer was holding back. "Can you tell us about the Maddox estate?"

Paladin's eyebrow shot up. "That depends on what you'd like to know."

Caroline frowned. "For starters, if the family is so wealthy, why is the estate in such disrepair?"

"That my dear, is a discussion you should have with your uncle. He manages the estate as well as the other real estate property owned by the Maddox trust."

Don had already figured this out while working on Samuel's huge personal portfolio. What wasn't clear was where Samuel had received the initial money for his own investing. Capital siphoned from his father's estate? A very good reason for wanting to get rid of his niece.

EIGHT

Paladin rose. "I'm sorry to cut this short, but I have a client coming in soon and need to prepare. You understand, of course."

"Of course," Don echoed, not getting a clear read on the man.

Caroline rose. "Thank you for your time, Mr. Paladin."

"My pleasure, Ms. Tully."

They left the law firm and headed back toward the rental car. The niggling feeling of observation trickled down Don's spine again. He pulled Caroline up short and searched for the cause of his unease. Frustration pounded at his temple when he couldn't find the source. He hurried Caroline to the car.

"We've one more stop before returning to the house," Don informed her as he snapped his seat belt in place.

"Where?"

"The sheriff's department."

He drove the few blocks to the other side of town and parked in the front of the brick building. The American flag and Mississippi state flag flew side by side from the pole in front of the main double doors. Inside the station house, the walls had been spruced up with fresh paint. Christmas decorations hung from the front desk as Don and Caroline stepped forward.

A man wearing a tan uniform like Sheriff Gantz's glanced up. "Help you, folks?"

"We'd like to see Sheriff Gantz," Don said. "This is Caroline Tully, Elijah Maddox's granddaughter."

The desk sergeant's eyes grew round. "Well, now. Doesn't that beat all? I'd heard a rumor the Maddox's secret heiress was in town, and now here you are in the flesh. I'll let the sheriff know you're here."

Small-town news traveled fast. They didn't have to wait long before Sheriff Gantz strode toward them.

He shook Don's hand and nodded a greeting to Caroline. "Let's talk in my office."

They followed him to a corner office. The windows overlooked the front walk. Only one chair faced the desk. Caroline sat while the sheriff rounded his desk and took a seat in his captain's chair. Don stood next to Caroline and placed a protective hand on her shoulder.

"I trust all is well and there haven't been any more incidents?" Sheriff Gantz said.

"No, no more intruders," Don answered. "We just came from Dr. Reese's office."

Gantz nodded. "I've had a talk with Doc Reese, as well. He's concerned about the slow progress Elijah is making. I suggested he pay his patient a visit soon."

"While we appreciate that, we plan to get a second opinion."

"That's a wise decision," the sheriff said. "Though I'm a bit confused why you're here."

"We're hoping you could help us find someone," Don

explained. "Isabella Maddox wrote in her diary about a man named Johnny. We don't have a last name."

"That's a common name." The sheriff looked at Caroline. "Do you think this Johnny is your father?"

"I don't know," she said, her voice breaking slightly. "There were two men in her life at the time of her death. One appears to have been my father, while the other…the other one frightened her. Maybe even threatened her. But she mentions only a name—Johnny— once, and it's not clear which man she means."

"I'll ask around, see if anyone can remember someone by the moniker of Johnny associated with Isabella."

Don shook the sheriff's hand. "We appreciate it, sir."

On the way back to the mansion, the sky opened up again and torrential rain pounded the rental car. Don flipped on the wipers to full blast. A few cars passed going toward town. Through the rearview mirror, the road behind them was clear.

"I don't like this weather," Caroline commented. "Give me a few feet of snow any day over this much rain."

"Spoken like a true New Englander."

A truck sat parked on the side of the road up ahead. The same model that had come at them the first day they'd arrived. Don tensed, but kept his speed even as they passed by the vehicle.

Don couldn't make out the driver's face beneath the brim of a ball cap and sunglasses. Caution seeped through Don's system. It *was* the same truck with the missing plates. The truck pulled out behind them and roared closer.

"Call 911," Don said, tossing his phone into her lap.

Caroline scooped up the cell phone and punched in

the numbers. A moment later, she was talking to an emergency operator.

The narrow, unfamiliar road was slick from rain and visibility limited. Don could just make out a side road coming up on the right.

"Hang on," Don said, as the speedometer inched higher.

The car hurtled forward. Don cranked the steering wheel and tapped the brake, intending to skid into the turn.

There was a second of tension in the pedal before it depressed all the way to the floor.

Brake failure!

Alarms flared inside Don. He stomped down on the emergency brake. Nothing. The car careened out of control.

Caroline screamed. The cell phone went flying, smacking against the dashboard and disappearing beneath the seat.

The back tires spun on the pavement, fighting for traction in the downpour, and lost. The rear fishtailed, and then whipped into a tailspin. Don yanked the steering wheel into the momentum of the spin until the back end and the front were lined up. He fought to straighten the steering wheel. The car shot off the road and bounced down an embankment, rumbled across underbrush before coming to a shuddering stop.

The truck chasing behind them overshot the turn and roared away in a spray of mud from the shoulder.

Don threw the gearshift into Park and turned to Caroline. "You okay?"

She shook her head. Her eyes were wide, the pupils dilated, her complexion pale. With a squawk, she fumbled with the door handle. The door popped open. She leaned out and threw up. Don's gut clenched with empathy. He reached over to gently rub her back until she sat upright.

Wiping her mouth with the back of her hand, she closed her eyes and leaned against the seat. "That was horrible."

"Yeah, it was."

The back window exploded in a cacophony of noise and flying glass.

Someone was shooting at them!

Reacting instantly, Don grabbed Caroline and forced her down to the floorboard. His mind ran the scenario. If they remained in the car, they were sitting ducks. All someone had to do was walk up to the car and blast away until they both were riddled with holes. He couldn't count on help arriving in time. He needed to act. Keeping low, he yanked the gearshift into Drive, twisted the steering wheel and stomped on the gas. The sedan spun in a whirl of velocity. Don held the wheel steady until the nose of the car faced the road. The tires spun but the car didn't move forward.

Frustration pounded in Don's ears. They'd have to take a stand. He powered down the side window and cut the engine. "Stay down."

"I'm not going anywhere!"

He yanked his weapon from his holster and flung his door open. Using the panel as cover, he climbed out. He racked the slide to chamber a round. The sound of metal grating on metal was barely audible above the tinging of rain pelting the car. Sighting down the barrel of his Glock, he searched for his target.

Movement. There. In the tree line about fifty yards

away on the other side of the main road, a man darted behind the trunk of a tree. An easy shot.

Steadying his hand, Don aimed, his finger touching the trigger and waited. He had to line this up just right to get an injury that would stop the man from running—and shooting—but wouldn't be so serious that he'd be unable to answer questions.

"Come on, come on," he muttered, impatient for the man to show himself again.

The blast of a rifle echoed in the air a split second before the thud of a bullet hit the door panel. The door bounced on its hinge. Don absorbed the impact and squeezed the trigger. His aim was true. A shout of pain burst from their assailant. The guy went down.

Caroline lifted her head. "I heard a scream."

"Yeah."

Don waited. He wasn't going to break cover until he was sure the guy was alone.

After several heartbeats, he said, "Caroline, crawl over here."

She scrambled across the driver's seat and crouched beside him.

"We're going over there," Don said. "I need you to stay right behind me."

She nodded.

In a low crouch, Don and Caroline left the safety of the car and made their way through the marshy grass toward the trees and the downed assassin.

A scrawny man lay at the base of a tree. Beneath his ball cap, his hawklike features stretched tight in obvious pain. Fear-filled eyes stared at Don. A crimson stain spread out from a wound in the guy's shoulder. Damage assessment quickly assured Don the bullet went clean through. No vital organs hit, just as he'd planned.

Don kicked aside the .22 long rifle, more appropriate for small-game hunting than a professional sniper's tool.

Which this guy clearly wasn't.

"You recognize him?" Don asked Caroline.

She shook her head. "No. I've never seen him before."

Not the man she'd seen hanging around her apartment and shop. Were the two incidents even related?

Bending close to the man lying on the ground, Don said, "Who hired you?"

"I'm not saying nothing until I have a lawyer," the guy ground out between clenched teeth. His gaze, defiant and fearful, darted between Don and Caroline.

"That line may work with the police, but I'm not the police," Don said as he raised his Glock and pressed it against the man's temple. Beside him, Caroline sucked in a gasp. "I'm going to ask you again, if you don't answer I'll put another bullet in you. Who hired you?"

The man blinked, fresh fear bubbling in his eyes. "I don't know."

Don chambered a round. The sound filled the air like a death knell.

"Don!"

He ignored Caroline's shocked gasp and concentrated on the man before him.

"Please." The man held up a hand as if to ward off a blow. "I really don't know. I never saw him."

"How did he contact you?"

"I got a call asking if I wanted to make a big wad of

dough. The money, instructions and a plane ticket to Boston came in the mail."

"What were the instructions?"

"To get rid of Caroline Maddox."

Caroline shifted, drawing the man's gaze. "You rigged my apartment door with explosives?"

The guy had the good grace to looked ashamed. "Yeah." His expression darkened. "But it didn't work the way the internet said it would."

Great. Just what the world needed, a psycho killer with downloadable bomb-making instructions.

"Your second bomb worked better."

"Huh? Second bomb?" The man squinted in what seemed like real confusion.

"The one that felled the oak at the Maddox estate."

"Wasn't me."

"You didn't break in and try to strangle Caroline?"

The guy shook his head. "Naw. Didn't think of that."

A siren wailed. Don knew he only had a few more seconds alone with the man to get whatever information he could. "How do you contact the man who hired you?"

"I don't. He or she contacts me."

"What?"

"Hey, man, I don't know if the boss is a man or woman. Whoever my contact is used one of those voice sensitizers like they use in the movies."

A voice-altering synthesizer could be operated remotely from a computer anywhere in the world. "How did you get paid?"

"I haven't yet, cuz I haven't done the job."

The squeal of tires announced the sheriff's arrival.

Don picked up the rifle and headed back toward the road with Caroline at his side.

"Hey, you can't just leave me here to die!"

"You'll live," Don muttered. Behind bars.

They may have neutralized one player, but the person behind the threat to Caroline was still out there. Don would protect her with his life.

And not because it was his job.

The next morning after breakfast, Don escorted Caroline to the kitchen in search of Mary. Abigail and the twins were sequestered in the parlor and Samuel had driven to work.

Caroline found Mary in the pantry, gathering items from the shelves.

"Good morning," Caroline said from the doorway and reached for the sack of flour the older woman held.

Mary gave them a tentative nod and relinquished her burden. "Morning."

"I was hoping I could help you. Maybe learn some of your fabulous recipes."

Wariness flooded Mary's face. "Mrs. Maddox wouldn't approve."

Caroline had thought Elijah was the one who ruled the house with an iron fist. But apparently Aunt Abigail had control issues as well. Interesting. "I need something to keep me busy."

Mary's gaze dropped. A slight smile curved her lips. "You're more than welcome to help out and learn."

Don drew Caroline aside. "Don't leave the kitchen until I return. I'm going to find Horace and use his satellite phone to arrange for a doctor from Jackson to drive out here and examine Elijah."

Grateful to him for so many reasons, she leaned in to place a quick kiss on his cheek. "Thank you."

He gave her a slight smile and left. Caroline shoved away the tiny bite of disappointment that he hadn't turned his head and captured her lips again. With a sigh, she turned her attention to Mary.

After Mary explained the evening's menu, she set Caroline up at the counter. Using a paring knife, Caroline chopped carrots for tonight's stew. She felt relieved, knowing that the man who'd tried to kill her was locked up securely in jail. She'd slept well last night. But she knew the reprieve was only temporary. The person who really wanted her dead was still out there.

When she'd left her room this morning she'd half expected to find Don camped out in front of her door. Her disappointment only lasted a moment, because the door across the hall had opened a second later as if he'd been waiting for her to come out. Seeing him had given her a jolt of pleasure that lasted all through breakfast.

"You can put those carrots right on into the pot," Mary instructed, gesturing toward the stove.

Caroline carried the cutting board full of chopped pieces to the stove and dumped the carrots into the boiling broth. Tantalizing aromas of sage, cumin and beef rose with the steam. Even though lunch was several hours away and breakfast had been filling, Caroline's mouth watered. She'd carefully monitored every item being used in the kitchen and hadn't found anything to suggest the food was being tainted in any way.

Mary gestured to the flour sitting on the counter. "We'll make some biscuits to go with the stew."

"Yum." Caroline had never met a carb she didn't like. Buttermilk, real butter, flour, eggs and water all mixed together to make thick dough. Caroline kneaded the mixture with her hands while Mary washed dishes at the sink.

"Mary, do you remember anyone by the name of Johnny in Isabella's life?"

The sharp sound of shattering glass drew a cry from Caroline. Memories flooded her, panic flared. Had someone taken another shot at her?

Her heart kicked. Her stomach clenched. She whipped around expecting to find a threat. Instead, a shaking Mary stared at the broken pieces of a dish in the sink.

Breathing out a sigh of relief, Caroline crossed to the older woman. "Mary? Have you hurt yourself?"

She took a shuddering breath. Her frightened, wide-eyed gaze ripped at Caroline. "Where did you hear that name?"

Anticipation sent little alert signals through Caroline's veins. Her pulse raced. "Isabella talked about a man named Johnny in her diary. Who was he?"

Mary shook her head, her gaze dropped back to the sink. After a silent beat, Caroline pressed, "Please, if you know something tell me."

"Only your mother ever called him that," Mary whispered.

"Who? Who was he?"

"There are some things best left alone, child."

Caroline gripped the older woman's hand. "Not in this instance. This Johnny person may by my mother's murderer."

Mary gasped. Her tear-filled eyes pleaded with Caroline as if willing her to understand. Her work-strengthened grip tightened painfully, her desperation clear. "No. No, he wasn't. He loved Isabella. And she loved him."

"Tell me. I need to know."

"Dennis Jonathan Finch was my son," Mary stated. "Your father."

Heart racing, Caroline stared at the older woman. Her grandmother. She hardly dared to believe it. "Are you sure?"

More tears filled Mary's eyes. "Yes. You're my grandchild."

Needing to sit, Caroline led Mary to the block table and cane-back chairs in the corner of the kitchen. "Why didn't you tell me this when I first arrived?"

Contrition drew lines around Mary's mouth. "They're both gone. I didn't see what good it would do to reveal that Dennis and Isabella had had a child. But now—I can't let you or anyone believe Dennis was a murderer."

Though Caroline understood, it didn't change the fact that Mary had withheld vital information. Information that could lead to catching Isabella's killer. And possibly give them a clue as to who was after Caroline. Just because Dennis/Johnny had loved her didn't mean he couldn't have killed her. Anger put a hard edge to her words. "Don't you think I deserved to know who my father was?"

Mary winced. "Yes, of course. It's just…"

"They'd been secret lovers?"

The older woman drew herself up. "I raised my son to believe in the sanctity of marriage and all that goes with it."

Shock siphoned the air from her head. "Are you saying they were married?"

Mary nodded. "They eloped. No one knew, except for me—and they didn't even tell me until afterward."

Grappling with this information, Caroline placed a hand on the older woman's arm. "Tell me about them?"

Mary wiped at her eyes. "Dennis was two years older than Isabella but they were best friends and grew up here together. Dennis, Isabella, Samuel and a few other local kids filled this house with laughter. Back then, everyone loved to come to the Maddox estate. Mrs. Maddox enjoyed having the children underfoot. And I think Mr. Maddox did as well even though he'd bluster that he didn't."

Caroline tried to imagine what it must have been like in this house back then. Light and laughter. Full of love.

The image didn't equate with the gloomy, oppressed place the estate had become.

Mary stared off toward the kitchen window, her expression softening as she recalled the past. "Dennis was a very jovial boy. Always seeking adventure. He joined the army when he turned eighteen."

Like Don. The thought darted across Caroline's mind.

"Two years later he came home with an injury. He'd jumped out of a helicopter and shattered his left leg. The doctors put him back together with pins. He limped after that and was honorably discharged. He was home in time to see Isabella graduate from high school. They had a summer romance."

Mary brought her gaze to Caroline. "You and your young man remind me of them. The way you two watch each other when the other isn't paying attention. The protective way Don is with you. The pink in your cheeks whenever he's near. I can tell how much in love you are. Just like Dennis and Isabella were." Her voice faded away, nodding sagely.

Caroline's throat constricted. Blood rushed to her head. In love? Her and Don? No. Ridiculous.

Fake fiancé, remember?

Mary saw what she and Don wanted people to see.

Did she really blush when he was near? That couldn't be faked.

"Unlike you two, though," Mary continued, drawing Caroline back to the conversation. Thankfully Mary wasn't aware how distressing her words were to Caroline. "Dennis and Isabella had to keep their feelings quiet, because they both knew Mr. Maddox wouldn't approve. He and the missus had grand plans for their daughter.

"Isabella had a mind of her own." Mary shook her head. "She applied to Tulane behind her daddy's back. Once she was accepted, Mr. Maddox couldn't persuade her not to go. Dennis stayed behind that fall, wanting to give her time to find herself, see who and what she wanted in life." A sad smile touched her lips. "At Christmas she came home claiming she wanted him and only him. Dennis was ecstatic. They took off one day and went to the next county over. They came back that evening married."

Caroline inhaled sharply. And her heart broke for the young couple. "Mr. Maddox found out, didn't he?"

"About the relationship. Not the marriage." Mary sighed, but Caroline didn't detect any anger. "He was livid. He wanted his daughter to marry within her own station in life, not settle for the help's son."

Searching the older woman's face for any sign of bitterness, Caroline said, "That must have made you and Horace very angry."

Mary looked in her in the eye. "Not angry so much as hurt. Or at least I was hurt. Horace agreed with Mr. Maddox. Dennis admitted to Horace that they'd gotten married, and he demanded Dennis get an annulment before Mr. Maddox discovered the truth."

It was all so unfair. "Why?"

"Our families are like oil and water. Coexisting, but separated. It's just the way it is."

Caroline understood what Mary was saying. As much as she didn't like isolating classes, she knew it was a reality all the same. Her best friend, Kristina, had almost lost the love of her life because of the division between her upscale upbringing and Gabe's blue-collar world.

Mary sighed. "Mr. Maddox and Isabella had a horrible argument. She returned to school and never came back. Dennis moved to New Orleans, took a job at a grocery store."

Caroline's chest ached with sadness and sympathy. "Where is Dennis now?"

Pain marched across Mary's face. "He died that winter. A hunting accident. He never knew he'd fathered a child. None of us knew until Mr. Elijah opened the box that led him to find you."

The news sliced deep. Her biological father was dead.

So much tragedy in this family. For a moment, Caroline was overwhelmed by the unfairness of it all, of her parents being taken from her before she had a chance to know them at all.

If Dennis had lived, he and Isabella would have

raised their child together. But then Caroline would never have known the love of her adoptive parents. A love that was given freely, because they'd wanted her so badly.

Something softened in her heart. Tears streamed down her cheeks. "I'm so sorry for your loss. Is Dennis buried in the same cemetery as Isabella?"

Mary nodded. "Isabella insisted that he be buried in the Maddox family plot. Mr. and Mrs. Maddox allowed it."

One mystery solved. Her father was Dennis Jonathan "Johnny" Finch. The love of Isabella Maddox's life.

But then who was the man Isabella had been afraid of? Was this man the one who had killed her? And was that man now after Caroline?

NINE

"Caroline, the doctor's here," Don said from the kitchen doorway.

Jolted out of her thoughts, Caroline nodded. Torn by her need to see to her grandfather's care and wanting to stay with...her grandmother, she hesitated.

Mary squeezed her hand. "Go on, child. See to Mr. Elijah. He needs you."

"I'll come back later," Caroline promised, her heart aching with sorrow.

As she and Don made their way toward the entry-way, Don halted her with a hand on her arm. "You look upset. What happened?"

Appreciating his concern and needing...to be held, to feel a connection with him, she hugged him tight. He stiffened for a moment then held her close, one hand pressing against her back, the other cradling her head. She held in the sob that threatened to escape. Instead, she focused on the warmth of Don's embrace, the spicy scent of his aftershave, the way his heart beat against her cheek. So comforting, so secure. So...

In love.

She squeezed her eyes tight, denying Mary's words parading around her head.

"What is it, sweetheart?"

Taking a shuddering breath, she lifted her gaze. "Mary and Horace are my paternal grandparents. Her son, Dennis Jonathan, was 'Johnny,' my father."

Surprise widened his blue eyes. "Where is he?"

She dropped her head back to his chest. "He died, months before I was born. He never knew about me."

He stroked her hair. "I'm so sorry."

The gentle tone of his voice, the soothing caresses of his hands made her melt. Clinging to him, she wished they could stay this way forever; just the two of them, letting the world fade away.

The sound of a clearing throat broke the sweet illusion of isolation and comfort.

Horace stood a few feet away. "The doctor is waiting."

Her other grandfather. Fresh tears spilled down her cheek.

"We're coming," Don said and slowly released Caroline.

She wiped at her eyes, trying to gather her composure. "Sorry."

Crooking a finger beneath her chin, he lifted her face. "No need to apologize. I'm here for you."

For now. But soon he wouldn't be. Soon his job of protecting her would be over. And she'd best remember that fact. They weren't in love. Not even close. Straightening her shoulders, she stepped away from him and headed down the hall.

The doctor had graying hair and kind brown eyes. He wore a plaid sports jacket and khaki pants. His left hand gripped the handle of a black bag. With his free hand, he shook hands with Caroline, then Don.

"Thank you, Dr. Smith, for coming on such short notice," Don said.

"Not at all. It was a pleasant drive out here."

Don and Caroline led the doctor to Elijah's room.

"Elijah, this is Dr. Smith from Natchez," Caroline said as she took his hand. "Will you let him examine you?"

Elijah nodded. His sunken eyes made her stomach drop. He appeared frailer than he had when she'd visited earlier in the day.

"Hello, Mr. Maddox, I'm Dr. Frank Smith. You can call me Frank." The doctor set his bag on the foot of the bed and removed his stethoscope. "Let's listen to your heart."

Leaving the doctor to do his work, she and Don stepped out into the hall. She leaned against the wall.

Don braced one arm on the wall next to her head. He trailed a knuckle down her cheek. "You've had a lot to take in since we've arrived."

"I'm a little shell-shocked," she admitted. "Sad, too."

"You're very brave and handling all of this very well."

She liked his praise. Liked the funny little tingles shooting off inside her, making her want to wrap her arms around him again. "Thank you."

"I call it like I see it," Don said.

Unable to resist, she placed a hand over his heart. "I appreciate that about you."

He captured her hand and brought her palm to his lips. His gaze bore into her. The light kiss he placed in the soft center of her hand made her mouth go dry. They were acting like they really were a couple in love.

But no one was watching. There was no need for the act.

Panicked because she was afraid of wanting this to be real, she quickly slipped away from him. "I'd like to visit my birth parents' graves."

He straightened, his expression shifting to neutral, making her think she'd imagined the yearning she'd seen in his Caribbean-blue eyes moments ago. "We can do that this afternoon."

They lapsed into silence. Though only a few feet separated them, she felt a chasm had opened up. She didn't like it at all.

Twenty minutes later, the doctor stepped out into the hall.

His grave expression sent shivers of alarm down Caroline's spine. "I concur with the Addison's diagnosis and the treatment plan that Dr. Reese has prescribed," Dr. Smith said. "But without further testing, I can't say why his disease is progressing so rapidly. I've taken blood samples and will run some additional diagnostics, but he should be admitted to a hospital today for observation until we can get a handle on the disease. I'll confer with Dr. Reese and let the hospital know to expect Mr. Maddox."

"I don't know if he'll agree to go, though," Caroline interjected.

"Then convince him." Dr. Smith turned his attention back to Don. "The hospital will arrange transportation. Please make sure to send along his medications with the paramedics."

"We will. Thank you, Doctor. We appreciate you coming out here." Don shook his hand.

"I can see myself out," Dr. Smith said when they moved to walk him down the stairs. "Go convince your grandfather that if he wants to live, he needs to go to the hospital."

Caroline's heart squeezed tight. Even though she'd only known Elijah for four days, she cared for him and didn't want him to die.

She squared her shoulders. "I will, Doctor."

"I don't like hospitals," Elijah groused for the umpteenth time.

"Elijah, the doctor says you need to go, so you're going," Caroline said with a firm tone.

Don was proud of her for sticking to her guns. She and Elijah had been going round and round for the past half hour while he and Horace communicated with the hospital and Samuel.

"Don't get cheeky with me, girl," Elijah said.

Caroline grinned. "If getting cheeky gets me what I want, then I'll get cheeky."

"Humph. You're more like your mother than I thought. She'd get cheeky, too."

"And I'll bet she got her way, too," Don interjected.

Pride tempered by sadness filled the old man's eyes. "Yes. She did."

"Elijah, why didn't you tell me you knew who my father was?" Caroline's voice dripped with emotion.

His eyes widened. "You know?"

She nodded. "Mary told me."

Elijah seemed to deflate. "I'm so ashamed that I objected to the relationship. Dennis was a fine boy."

Don slipped an arm around Caroline. For a split second she held herself still, then relaxed against his side. "Then why did you disapprove?"

Tears spilled down his cheeks. "It was foolish of me. My biggest regret. If I hadn't…" The unspoken words hung in the air.

Don couldn't imagine living with the pain and regret echoing in Elijah's tone. It made him think of his own father. Did he feel remorse for leaving his wife and child? Did he have any idea of the damage he'd caused? The pain he'd inflicted?

Was he even alive?

Don forced him from his mind as he bolstered his own vow never to be like his father. To never hurt the one who loved him. And the only way to do that was to never allow anyone to love him.

Everything inside him tensed with anxiety. With Caroline melding into his side like two halves of a whole perfectly fitted together it was hard to want to disconnect. But he had to be careful with her. For her sake, he had to keep their relationship strictly professional. He'd done a poor job of it so far. He eased away from her, determined to keep an arm's length between them.

Steering the conversation in a new direction, he said, "We haven't found the secret passages you talked about. Can you tell us where they are?"

Elijah shook his head. "I've never seen them. But I know they exist. My father used them."

For the next two hours, Elijah regaled them with tales of his childhood. His conviction that there were tunnels through the house never wavered. When the paramedics arrived they made short work of moving

Elijah into the back of the vehicle. The family stood on the porch as the ambulance carrying Elijah rumbled down the drive.

Samuel followed the ambulance in his Bentley. He'd come home from work to accompany his father. When Don had called him to inform him they were sending Elijah to the hospital, Samuel had sounded relieved. Which made Don wonder why Samuel hadn't made these arrangements sooner. Sheriff Gantz assured Don he'd post a guard outside Elijah's room.

"He'll be miserable there," Abigail sniffed. She'd made her disapproval known the instant she'd be told about the move. With a parting glare, she stormed inside and a moment later a door slammed shut.

The twins turned accusing eyes toward Caroline.

"What if he dies in that hospital?" Lilly said, tears welling in her hazel eyes. "He should be here with us."

"He's not going to die," Caroline said, her voice full of empathy. "He'll be back soon, better than ever."

Don hoped she was right, for all their sakes.

"Come on, Lilly, no use standing here moping," Landon said, clearly trying to be the strong one. "Grandfather wouldn't approve."

Caroline shook her head as the kids left. "I know we did the right thing, but I feel bad for them. They really love him."

"They'll be fine once Elijah is well." He caught himself starting to slip his arm around her. He stepped away and jammed his hands into his pants pockets. "You said you wanted to visit Dennis's and Isabella's graves."

"Yes, I do."

Her pleased, grateful look sent the urge to reach for

her again spiraling through him. He fisted his hands and forced himself to stand down.

Mary had given them directions to the cemetery. They headed through the woods south of the house beneath a sky gray and hazy. The temperature dropped a few degrees, making coats necessary. Borrowed rain boots made little noise on the wet carpet of fallen leaves, soggy grasses and muddy earth.

Caroline and Don cleared the woods and came out on the edge of the cemetery. Caroline could see that the lawns, though strewn with fresh debris from the storm, were obviously cared for. Aged-stone grave markers, ranging from simple to ornate, dotted the landscape, each free from moss or decay beyond the normal ravages of time.

"Who keeps this so nicely maintained?" she asked.

"There must be a hired caretaker."

He was right of course. It seemed odd that the Maddox family estate would languish in disrepair while the family plots were tended to so meticulously.

On the far side of the cemetery was an entrance and road leading off into the distance. A lonely feeling infused Caroline. She tried to shake it as they walked along the headstones reading the names.

Caroline lurched to a stop when she came across a Maddox name. She read aloud. "Gideon Maddox. 1882–1951. This must be Elijah's father."

"Your great-grandfather."

Wonder filled Caroline. All around her was evidence of ancestors whose DNA she shared. But she lacked any history with them. She didn't belong here. "By blood. But can I really claim this family when I've never known them?"

Her family was in New Hampshire. Her history was with the Tullys.

She moved down the row of gravesites, spotting Isabella's.

"You have a chance to know some of the Maddoxes now."

Don's softly spoken words lanced through her as she dropped to her knees in front of Isabella's headstone. "Ever since I was little I never felt like I belonged anywhere. Don't get me wrong, my parents are great and I love them dearly." She hadn't realized how much until coming to Mississippi. "But sometimes...I wondered who my birth mother was, why she gave me away. Was there something wrong me?"

Don crouched beside her. "There's nothing wrong with you."

The fierceness of his tone touched her, made her believe he cared for her and not just because she was paying him to. She wasn't sure she was ready to look closely at what that could mean for her, for them.

Mary's words echoed in her head. *In love. In love.*

She traced Isabella's name in the cold stone focusing on the tactile sensation. "I know she did what she thought was best. But I can't help wonder if she'd kept me, if she'd told her parents about me...how much different our lives would have been."

"We'll never know. Nothing good will come from spinning your wheels, trying to imagine." His resigned tone made it clear he spoke from experience.

She lifted her gaze to him. "Your father?"

"I wanted him to come back in the worst way. Imagined every sort of scenario. Him walking through the front door. Him appearing at one of my soccer games.

Him showing up at my high-school graduation." He shook his head. "I learned that it's better not to imagine and dream. Hurts less."

Understanding flooded her. They shared a common bond. "When Cullen first died, I would sit for hours just staring at the walls wondering and imagining what the future would have been like if he hadn't died." The pain of those days scored her, as fresh now as then. Her mouth twisted as anger stirred. "But then I found out…"

His eyes sharpened. "You found out what?"

"His 'friend.'" She made quote marks with her fingers. "The one he went skiing with—was a woman. They were having an affair." Bitterness laced her words, clogged her throat.

Don winced. "How did you find out?"

"Someone let it slip at the funeral." She gave a humorless laugh, remembering how the humiliation and betrayal had cut so deep she marveled she still had any blood left after such brutal wounds. "I was such a fool."

"No!" Don wrapped his arms around her. "*He* was."

She settled her head against his chest and took solace in his closeness, accepting his comfort for what it was, not what she wished it could be. "I actually confronted her."

She hadn't told anyone about this. Not even her parents. "She didn't deny their relationship." Her hands fisted. "I don't understand how he could have done this to me. If he didn't love me anymore, why not just break our engagement off instead of leading me on, thinking I would be spending the rest of my life with him?"

"You haven't forgiven him," he stated in a hushed tone.

She squeezed her eyes tight. "No. I can't."

Don tightened his arms around her. Anger that the jerk would hurt her sliced through him, leaving a burning wound. He kissed the top of her head. The fresh fragrance of apple shampoo teased his senses. She shifted slightly, making him aware of all her soft curves pressing close.

He wished he could make her hurt go away. Like he'd wished he could heal his mother's wounds when his father walked out. But he couldn't.

He could only make sure he never hurt anyone like that. Including the beautiful woman within his embrace. But he couldn't bring himself to release her. Not yet.

The scuff of feet snapped him to attention. The sensation of being watched itched along his skin. Caution raced through his pulse. He scanned the cemetery and the tree line beyond. Nothing. He was getting sick of this cat-and-mouse game. This needed to end. But he couldn't leave Caroline's side.

"We should get back," he stated, wary of how vulnerable they were out in the open. If another hired gunman were taking aim right now—

"Don, what is it?" The anxiety in her voice matched the alarm ricocheting through his system.

"I have a bad feeling." He pulled his sidearm from his ankle holster. "Let's go."

Don kept a vigilant watch as they headed back through the trees. The forest took on an ominous feel. Shifting shadows grated on Don's nerves. His muscles tensed. Every sense quivered with high alert.

Up ahead a shadow moved. Not just the shifting of

leaves and branches. A man lurked beneath a massive angel oak tree.

"Hey! Don't move," Don yelled and fired a warning shot.

The guy dove for the cover of a blackberry bramble, then crashed through to the other side. He ran through the woods toward the road that ran west of their position.

Caroline pushed at Don, urging him to move. "Go! Get him!"

The need to act galvanized him. "Stay out of sight. I'll be back."

Determined to neutralize the threat once and for all, Don crashed through the underbrush after the man.

Heart pounding in her ears, Caroline crouched behind the thick trunk of the angel oak tree. Softly she prayed, "Please, Lord, let him catch this guy without having to shoot him."

The memory of the last man Don had gone after surfaced. The blood. The sound of the slide of Don's gun. The fierce look on his face. A warrior. A protector. The man she was rapidly falling for despite her best intentions not to. The world tilted as the realization reverberated around her head and her heart.

An out-of-place noise overtook the rush of blood in her head.

Dogs' vicious barking. Getting closer. Louder. Angrier.

Two dark splotches crashed through the underbrush. Sharp teeth gleamed from snarling canine mouths.

She jumped up to reach a low-hanging branch. She struggled to hug the branch, the sleeve of her shirt catching. She felt a stinging pain on her arm as she swung her feet up, barely escaping the snapping jaws of two sleek Dobermans.

"Shh. Nice doggies," she said, transfixed by the creatures.

Her breath lay trapped in her lungs and her muscles ached from holding on to the branch. For several long, agonizing minutes she hung in the air while the dogs barked, jumped, circled the tree and jumped some more. The animals seemed impervious to the rain that began to fall. Water dripped down Caroline's back where her rain jacket gapped, but she couldn't do anything about it except endure more discomfort.

"Felix! Oscar!"

Caroline had never been so happy to hear her uncle's voice.

Samuel Maddox skidded to a halt, his eyes growing round as he gaze bounced between the dogs and Caroline.

"Fuss!" he commanded, the words sounding foreign and having no meaning to Caroline. *"Platz."*

Immediately, the dogs dropped to their bellies. The barking ceased. The quiet was unnerving.

Caroline stared at her uncle. "What did you say to them?"

"The dogs are trained in German. *Fuss* means heel, *Platz,* down."

The words sounded more like *foos* and *plots,* but whatever, they got the job done.

"I'm so sorry, my dear," Samuel said, reaching up for her. "Let me help you down."

She clung to the branch, not willing to trust the dogs. "They look like they want to eat me."

He let out an exasperated breath. "They won't hurt you unless they feel threatened."

Her arms began to shake, her hold weakening. "I'm good here."

"Nonsense. You could fall and hurt yourself."

She readjusted her grip. The bark of the tree was becoming increasingly slippery. She wouldn't be able to hold on much longer. Did she dare trust her uncle? Don was convinced Samuel was the one behind the attempts on her life.

Her grip slipped. She let out a gasp as her feet lost their hold and swung away from the branch to dangle above the ground.

The dogs snarled.

"Nein!" Samuel snapped.

He placed his hands lightly around her waist and helped her safely to the ground. "There now." He stepped back. "What are you doing out here?"

Keeping an alert eye on the dogs, she answered, "Don and I were visiting the cemetery."

Understanding dawned. "Ah." He looked around. "Where's Don?"

"There was a man watching us. Don chased after him."

Alarm flared in Samuel's eyes. Real or pretend? "That's not good."

Not it wasn't. She pointed to the animals at her uncle's feet. "Where did they come from?"

He frowned. "I'd just returned from the hospital and noticed someone had opened the kennel. I heard the barking and came as quickly as I could." He shook his head. "I don't know why they came after you. They normally don't attack people unless provoked."

"I guess I'm special," she muttered. "Thank you for coming to my rescue."

"My dear," Samuel said, leveling her with a grave look. "It might be better for you to leave before something bad happens to you."

Tired of being scared, she planted her hands on her hips. "*Something bad.* Is that a threat? Are *you* the one trying to kill me?"

TEN

"Kill you?" Samuel's eyes went wide with confusion. "Why on earth would I want to do that?"

Caroline arched an eyebrow and fought down the uneasiness that came from confronting a man who might very well want her dead. "Because with me out of the way you'd inherit everything."

"No! I wouldn't hurt you." He shook his head grimly. "But I do worry for you. Did you know that members of our family tend to meet with tragic ends? I would hate for anything to happen to you."

Unconvinced his advice to leave wasn't meant in a more sinister way, she asked, "You mean Isabella's death?"

He nodded. "Isabella. Great-grandfather, Uncle Gerome, my mother. Now my father." He heaved a suffering sigh. "The Maddoxes are cursed with tragic ends."

A shiver of unease tripped down her spine. "Your father isn't dead yet, Samuel."

He waved her off in a way that implied "soon enough." "Don't you think dying of disease is tragic?"

She grimaced. Yes, she did. Unfortunately, sickness

was part of the human condition. "How did the others die?"

"Great-grandfather fell down a well. He was there three days before they discovered him. Uncle Gerome died in a plane crash in the Andes. My mother had a heart attack. I only wonder what tragic end God has in store for me." He seemed resigned to his fate.

Hoping she wasn't making a mistake by allowing compassion to temper her guard, she reached out to gently touch his arm. "Uncle Samuel, God doesn't plan tragic deaths." It hurt her heart to think he'd assign some sort of blame to God for the randomness of life. "None of us know how we'll go or when. What matters is the life we live while we're here."

His eyes misted. He patted her hand. "Bless you, child. You remind me so much of Isabella. She would have thought the same. She had a deep faith in God. I know she struggled at times as we all do. But I know she's in Heaven smiling down on us."

Thinking of her mother in God's embrace warmed Caroline's heart and solidified her determination to get to the bottom of the threat to her and her grandfather's lives. She prayed Samuel wasn't the bad guy. But if not him, then who? And why? Was it tied to Isabella's murder, and the man who killed her?

So many questions could drive a person to distraction.

There was a rustling sound nearby, and the dogs let out a vicious growl, startling Caroline back a step.

The dogs jumped to their feet and barked but didn't leave Samuel's side as two sets of footsteps drew closer.

"Nein!" Samuel commanded. The dogs stopped barking, but remained at attention, their beady black

eyes on Don and his prize as they emerged through the trees.

Looking disheveled from his chase and decidedly angry, Don approached with a man held in a tight grip. Caroline gasped. She recognized Don's captive's angular features and shaggy blond hair. He didn't look nearly as big and threatening as he had in Boston beneath a trench coat and fedora.

"What is going on?" Samuel questioned. "Willard, what were you doing out here on the back property spying on my niece and her fiancé?"

Don shoved the man forward. "You know this guy?"

"He's a private detective. My father hired him to find Caroline."

"That's the man I saw loitering around my apartment building and shop in Boston," Caroline explained.

"Willard, what do you have to say for yourself?" Samuel asked.

Giving Caroline a caustic glare, he said, "I came to the house to talk to Mr. Maddox, but then I saw these two sneaking off into the woods. I thought I should see what they were up to."

"We weren't sneaking off," Caroline snapped.

"Why did you want to speak with Mr. Maddox?" Don asked.

"I haven't been paid for finding the secret Maddox heiress. Mr. Paladin said I wouldn't be paid until after January. But I need the money now."

Don narrowed his gaze. "Did Paladin say why he wouldn't pay until after the New Year?"

Willard jerked his shirtsleeves straight in a vain effort to restore order to his appearance. "He was being right stubborn about it. Said Mr. Maddox had stipulations that needed to be met before any money would be released. So I came to talk with Mr. Maddox myself. I didn't agree to any stipulations."

Caroline exchanged a glance with Don and saw her thoughts reflected in his eyes. The stipulation was she had to stay through New Year's Day. But why would that affect payment of the P.I. who'd tracked her down?

"Come along, Willard, I'll make sure you're paid for services rendered," Samuel said as he started walking toward the estate, the dogs at his heels.

Willard shot Don a wary glance before hustling after Samuel like one of his pets.

Don grasped Caroline's wrist and held her arm up. "What happened?"

She glanced at her forearm. Blood soaked the cuff of her jacket sleeve. Surprise rocked through her. She pulled the material back to reveal deep scrapes on her forearm.

She made a face. "Felix and Oscar happened. Remember the dogs we heard barking?"

Don shot a glare at the retreating Dobermans and their master. "Samuel and I are going to have chat." He turned back to her, self-recrimination clear in his expression. "I shouldn't have left you."

"You did the right thing. If you hadn't caught Willard, we'd still think someone was gunning for me."

"Someone still is. I'm sure Samuel hired yesterday's shooter. He may have set the dogs after you hoping they'd do the job the bullets failed to do."

An anxious flutter hit her stomach. "I confronted Samuel. Asked him point-blank if he was the one trying to hurt me."

"What?" Don jabbed the air with his hand. "That was foolish. What if he'd done something?"

"But he didn't. I just don't buy that he's behind it all."

"For your sake, I hope you're right. But whether Samuel was behind it or not, someone still sent that hit man after you. You're still in danger. Please, don't do anything like that again."

"I won't. I promise." She frowned. "Samuel said that Felix and Oscar don't attack unless provoked. So why would they come after me?"

"That's a good question." He took her by the arm. "Let's inspect their kennel. Hopefully, we'll find the answer."

A mesh steel fence cordoned off the farthest edge of the property. Scattered hay soaked up the moisture from the rain and provided a hard-packed floor. In the center of the fenced area was a free-standing, very large doghouse. Felix and Oscar paced back and forth along the dog pen's edge, barking frantically as Don and Caroline approached. Samuel exited through a high metal gate.

"Anything out of place?" Don asked.

"Other than the door being wide open when I arrived and the dogs gone, no, nothing."

Don took each word with a grain of distrust. Of course he would claim nothing suspicious. "Where's Willard?"

Samuel sighed. "I sent him on his way with a check."

Don glanced at the growling dogs. "Who else will the dogs respond to?"

Samuel frowned. "You don't think someone deliberately sent the dogs to attack Caroline do you?"

"Maybe."

"A handful of people. Why would anyone do that?"

Don could think of a few million reasons. Greed did funny things to people.

Caroline moved closer to the fence, her gaze riveted on something. She pointed to a scrap of shredded material half buried beneath the hay. "That's my shirt."

Don stepped along side of her. "Now we know why the dogs came after you. Someone deliberately sent them into attack mode and gave them your scent."

Samuel went back inside the pen and retrieved Caroline's blouse, the one she'd worn the day they arrived.

Horror filled Samuel's face as he held it up. "I'm so sorry, Caroline. I don't know how that got in there."

Don pinned him with a pointed look. "Someone has been trying to prevent Caroline from claiming her inheritance since she learned about it."

Samuel's gaze jumped between Caroline and Don. "It's not me."

Don crowded him. "You're the only one who has anything to gain."

Not shrinking away, Samuel turned to Caroline. "My dear, I wouldn't ever try to hurt you," he said with a plea in his voice. "Isabella was my sister. I loved her. As her child, you're entitled to everything she would have inherited. I would never stand in the way of that. You must believe me."

Irritated not to find a hint of guilt in the older man, Don's jaw tightened. If Samuel wasn't involved, then Don didn't have any idea who was.

Caroline put a firm, restraining hand on Don's arm and addressed her uncle. "Why didn't you tell us about Dennis?"

Puzzlement twisted Samuel's face. "Dennis? Do you mean Dennis Finch?

She nodded. "Yes. Dennis Jonathan Finch."

Titling his head to the side, he asked, "What does he have to do with this? He died a long time ago."

"Did you know my mother called him Johnny?"

For a long moment Samuel stared, his face paling. "I'd forgotten. She only did that when we were children."

A faint smile touched Caroline's lips. "They fell in love the summer before Isabella went to college."

Clearly upset, Samuel rubbed his chin. "I didn't know."

"He was one of the men Isabella wrote about in her diary," Don said.

Samuel blinked. "What are you saying?" Then realization flared. "You think he was the man harassing her?"

Don put a protective arm around Caroline. "No. He was Caroline's father."

Samuel inhaled sharply. "How can you be sure?"

"Mary thinks it's true," Caroline answered. "But a DNA test would confirm."

Appearing genuinely shocked, Samuel said, "This is a lot to absorb."

"Yes, it is," Caroline agreed ruefully.

"That's good news indeed," Caroline said to the duty nurse on the other side of the call. "Thank you so much."

Caroline pressed the end button on the satellite phone, which looked more like a giant walkie-talkie than the normal cell phones she was used to, and handed it back to Don. "The nurse says Elijah's improving."

"Glad to hear it." He set the phone on the shelf of the bookcase he was inspecting. They were downstairs in the library, searching for the hidden passageways Elijah insisted were built into the house. Everyone else had gone upstairs to bed, leaving them free to probe. So far they'd come up empty on finding anything to suggest there were secrets inside the house's walls but she wasn't giving up. Outside the wind howled. Rain tapped against the window.

Moving behind her uncle's desk, she gently rapped her knuckles against the wall. "Now if they could only figure out what had been making him so ill."

"I'm sure the doctors will do their best." He removed a stack of books from the shelf and ran a hand over the back of the case. "He's where he needs to be right now. Whoever wants him dead can't get to him now."

"True." She lowered her voice. "I really want to believe Uncle Samuel isn't the one trying to kill Elijah or me."

"Maybe he's not. But remember, he could be a good actor. He has a compelling motive."

"This all seems so surreal, you know. From the moment I received the letter claiming I was an heiress I've felt like I've entered some sort of bizarre alternate reality."

He glanced over his shoulder and met her gaze. "You're not alone."

Staring into his handsome face, her heart squeezed tight. She'd invited Don to enter her bizarre world. She was thankful he kept her from falling apart. "No, I'm not."

Unfortunately, her bodyguard occupied more of her thoughts than was wise. His protection though needed and wanted was beginning to make her sad. It wouldn't last forever. Eventually, the danger would be resolved, she'd return to her life and he'd move on to protect someone else.

She didn't want to think about not having him in her life. He'd become her friend, her confidant. The person she turned to with her questions and heartache. The one she longed to share joy with.

But was she ready to take a risk on love again?

She honestly didn't know.

Late that night, Caroline moved restlessly about her bedroom, trying to calm herself enough to lie down. The search of the library had proved fruitless. So had every other place they'd checked—the parlor when the family was in their rooms. The kitchen when Mary and Horace were otherwise occupied. All to no avail. No secret passages to be found.

Finally, she sat at the vanity and smoothed a brush through her hair, hoping the rhythmic strokes would relax her. She listened to the way the house settled. Creaks and groans of boards shifting as the late-December temperature plummeted. A cold snap had charged through the South over the past twelve hours. A chill tripped up Caroline's spine. She'd grown accustomed to the more mild temperatures.

Finding no peace in brushing her hair, she set the brush down, rose and moved to the bed. If she lay down and tried some of the relaxation techniques she'd once read about in a magazine, maybe that would help. The article had listed ways to clear the mind, to relax the muscles. Blowing out a breath, she fluffed the pillow and then pulled back the covers.

She gasped.

A brown and yellow striped ribbon lay curled in the middle of the stark white sheets.

Caroline frowned as her mind grappled with the sight. In a split second, her mind clicked like pieces of a puzzle snapping together. That wasn't a ribbon.

It was a snake!

The creature moved. Lifted its head and slowly undulated, uncurling.

Panic shot through her, making her shake. Her breath hitched. She stumbled backward.

The creature slithered back beneath the covers until only the tip of its tail was visible.

"Don!" She bolted for the door. She'd barely got the lock undone before he burst in. She threw herself into his arms.

His blue-green eyes searched her face. So much compassion, so much worry. All for her. It made her feel as if she'd come…home.

"What happened?" he asked.

"Snnnake." She pointed to the bed. "In the bed."

"Let's get you out of here." He hustled her out of the room and into his.

"But the snake! What if it crawls off the bed and disappears into the house?"

"I'll take care of it."

A shudder ripped over her. "Please be careful."

He nodded and shut the door. Caroline hugged her arms around her middle and rocked. She hated creepy crawling things.

A few minutes later, Don returned. Anger etched lines in his face. "I'm going to wring those kids' necks."

"You think Landon and Lilly put the snake in my bed?"

"I do. They want to scare you off."

They'd made no secret of their wish that she'd leave. But to go so far as to put a snake in her bed? But then again, Don believed Landon and Lilly had set off the smoke bomb. Would the kids' pranks get out of hand? "Was it a poisonous snake?"

"No. It's a garden snake. Very typical of this area according to Horace."

Ripples of distaste cascaded over her flesh anyway. "What did you do with it?"

"Horace took it outside."

Grateful for that, she said, "I can't sleep in there now."

"I'll take that room. You can sleep here."

She didn't want him to leave the room but forced a nod.

"Thank you."

He cupped her cheek. "Don't worry. I'm not going to let anything happen to you."

She believed him. Trust and affection pushed back her fright. She planted her hands on his T-shirt-clad chest. "What would I do without you?"

He blinked. His expression shuttered. He dropped his hand away from her face. "Once you no longer need a bodyguard, you'll do fine without me."

His words couldn't have brought her back to reality any more effectively if they had been an ice-water spray in the face. "Right."

She shifted away. She had to stop herself from going

down this path. Don wasn't a permanent fixture in her life. He was only here temporarily because she'd hired him, not because he cared about her. Indulging in any fantasies of them being together was a chump's game.

The sooner her heart came to terms with that fact, the better.

What would I do without you?

Don struggled to come to terms with the way Caroline's words made him feel.

A deep-seated fear rose to taunt him. His mother had said similar words to his father before he'd walked out. The memory burned a hole through Don's consciousness. For years he'd replayed that fateful day when he'd been twelve, wishing there was some way to alter the outcome. Don had hid in the hall closet when the fighting started again. This time it seemed particularly bad. His mother screamed at his father. His father screamed back. Something smashed against the wall, the sound of breaking glass shuddering through Don. He'd heard his father's voice, heard the words "I can't take this anymore. I'm done."

His mother sobbed. "What will we do without you?"

"You'll figure it out."

The slam of the door echoed in the silence of the quiet house in the aftermath of the fight.

Don had emerged from the closet to find his mother crumpled on the floor, weeping. And his father gone.

He'd promised himself he'd never hurt anyone like that.

Don didn't want to be like his father.

Abiding by the rules and keeping everyone at a distance was the only way to ensure he never buckled under the pressure of responsibility.

Only when it came to Caroline, he couldn't seem to remember the rules.

Keeping Caroline at an emotional distance was the only way to protect her, no matter how wrong it felt. Giving in to the feelings she stirred, the longings for the kind of life normal people, well-adjusted people enjoyed would only lead to disaster.

He carried too much baggage, too much fear. She'd been hurt deeply once in her life by a man she loved. Don would never put her in jeopardy of being hurt again.

Not by him.

The next morning, Caroline entered the kitchen and saw Mary sitting at the pine table in the corner. "Good morning. What are you doing?"

A blustery wind blew through the trees and buffeted the house, making the windows rattle.

Mary lifted her gaze and smiled a welcome. "Come, I'd like to show you these pictures of Dennis."

She gestured to the many photos laid out across the tabletop in front of her, some yellowed and curling at the edges.

Heart hammering in her chest, Caroline sat in an empty chair. She picked up a photo of a young man in a military uniform. Her biological father. There was a resemblance between them in the line of his eyes and the shape of his jaw.

"Here are some of your mother, too."

Setting the picture she held aside, Caroline reached for the one Mary pointed to. The image captured a group of six kids mugging for the camera. Uncle Samuel and Dennis, she recognized. And her mother, with her dark hair plaited into two braids and wearing a wide smile. The others looked vaguely familiar. One boy was taller, older than the rest. Another boy had a sickly look about him, his skin pale and his blond hair cut short. The other girl in the photo was younger with long white-blond hair. "Who are the others?"

Mary tapped the image. "Randy. Abby. Georgie."

Caroline studied the photo. "Is this Aunt Abigail?"

"Yes. She had her sights set on Samuel way back then."

Confused, Caroline said, "I had the impression she wasn't from around here. She certainly doesn't sound Southern."

Mary laughed. "No, she doesn't. Her family moved here when she was six or seven, maybe."

Caroline picked up another photo. Two men dressed in hunting gear, arms slung around each other's shoulder, smiles spread from ear to ear. She stared. "Is this Mr. Paladin with Dennis?"

Leaning over to look, Mary nodded. "It is."

Caroline compared this photo to the group shot. Paladin was the sickly boy with Isabella and Dennis. Her pulse spiked as an inkling of unease slithered through her. "Didn't you tell me Dennis died on a hunting trip?"

Sadness darkened Mary's eyes. "That's correct. Dennis, Randy and Georgie had gone up north to hunt deer."

Bracing herself for the horrible details, she asked, "What happened?"

"They were twenty-five feet up in a hunting perch.

Dennis leaned too far out to get a shot off and fell to the ground. He died instantly."

The unease turned to full-fledged suspicion. She stared at the photos, her mind ticking through thoughts in rapid fire.

He fell? Or was he pushed?

Could one of these other two men be the man who'd stalked and killed her mother?

The questions screamed across her mind with all the velocity of a fighter jet, leaving a trail of anxiety in its wake.

Caroline needed to talk to Don. She pointed back to the group shot. "Who is this other kid?" she asked, surprise to hear her voice shake.

"Georgie? George Gantz."

Her breath caught. "The sheriff?"

"That's right."

Caroline scrambled to her feet, clutching the photos. "Do you mind if I show these to Don?"

"Of course not."

Caroline rushed from the kitchen in search of Don. If what she was thinking was true, they may finally have a lead as to who killed her mother.

But were either of these men involved in the threats against her life? And if so, why?

ELEVEN

Two hours later, Don parked the borrowed Bentley in front of Paladin's office. "We can't go in accusing him."

Caroline nodded, but he could tell she was itching to do just that.

Don agreed the photos were interesting and led to more questions. Such as, why if they were such close friends, Paladin hadn't known that Isabella called Dennis "Johnny." Seemed like something a good buddy would know. Unless he'd lied.

Don held open the door to Paladin's office for Caroline, then followed her inside. The receptionist wasn't at her desk.

"Hello?" Caroline called out.

Don knocked on the closed door to Paladin's private office. When no one answered, he pushed the door open, automatically careful not to disturb any fingerprints. Trent Associates were well trained in basic investigative protocol, regardless of their backgrounds. No one was inside.

"Seems odd to leave the offices unlocked and unmanned," Caroline remarked as she brushed past him to enter the room.

He made a gentle grab for her but missed. "I'm sure they'll return."

She nodded as she picked up one of the small, framed photos sitting on the credenza. When she looked up, excitement brightened her pretty eyes. "Look at this."

She held the picture out for his inspection. It was a formal photo of a family of four. A distinguished-looking man in a dark suit and tie sat in the center of the group, his resemblance to his son very clear. A woman with blond, upswept hair smiled at the camera. Paladin as a teen stood to his mother's right while a younger girl, sporting braces and white-blond pigtails on the other side of her father.

Stunned, Don's gaze met Caroline's. "Abigail."

"Abigail and—Paladin," Caroline confirmed. "I wonder why Mary didn't mention Aunt Abigail and Mr. Paladin are siblings."

Don wasn't sure how all the dots were lining up, but they still had another person to talk to. "Let's go see Sheriff Gantz."

Ten minutes later, they were ushered into the sheriff's office.

"I was planning on paying you a visit today," the sheriff said without preamble. "Please have a seat."

Caroline sat. Don remained standing. "You were coming out to the estate?"

"I was." Gantz opened a large manila envelope lying on his desk and dumped out two plastic, sealed evidence bags. Each bag contained an amber prescription bottle.

Caroline leaned forward. "What are those?"

"The medications that were sent to the hospital with

Elijah. The pills inside are salt pills. Easily bought over the counter and switched out for the real medicine."

"Someone has been tampering with Elijah's medication. No wonder his health hadn't been improving." Don gestured to the bottles. "Prints?"

Gantz shrugged. "None unexpected. Mary and Horace Finch. Abigail and Samuel Maddox. And yours, Ms. Tully."

Caroline sat back. "I handled the bottles when I gave them to the paramedics."

Gantz nodded. "I figured as much."

"Have you questioned the others?" Don asked.

"Not yet, but I intend to. I suggest keeping Mr. Maddox in the hospital until the culprit is found."

"I totally agree," Don stated.

"Can either of you think of a motive for someone to want Mr. Maddox dead?"

"His money," Don ventured.

"Or—" Caroline stared up at him. The anguish in her eyes tore him. "Mary and Horace have a reason."

"What reason?" Gantz demanded.

Don explained, "Elijah disapproved of Dennis and Isabella's relationship."

Gantz frowned. "Relationship?"

"Dennis Finch is my biological father," Caroline announced.

The sheriff sat back, clearly stunned by her words.

"Maybe this is some sort of revenge on Mary and Horace's part," Don said, his gaze on Caroline. Even though she was the one who'd brought up the possibility, it was clear she didn't want to believe it.

"But why now?" Caroline's eyebrow furrowed with confusion. "Why wait all these years?"

"Elijah became ill and they saw an opportunity. Hate can fester."

She shook her head. "Horace agreed with Elijah."

"But Mary?"

"I guess." Caroline appeared like she was going to be sick.

Empathy knotted in Don's gut. He could only imagine how upsetting this was.

"Wait a second." Gantz held up a hand. "You've lost me. Start at the beginning."

Don quickly filled in the pieces of the story that they knew.

"You're saying that the man your mother wrote about in her diary, the man she loved, was Dennis Finch?" Sheriff Gantz asked with puzzlement in his eyes. "Dennis and Isabella?"

"Why is that hard to believe?" Don asked, studying the man, looking for some hint of subterfuge.

"Dennis never said a thing to me." Gantz tapped a finger against his chin, his gaze taking on a faraway glaze. "Now it makes sense, though."

"What does?" Don asked.

"The day Dennis died, he'd hinted that he had come home from New Orleans for a rare visit because he had some news to tell us. But then we got caught up in the hunt and he never told us his news."

"He died before he could." *Which news was he going to tell his two best friends?* Don wondered. Was Dennis going to tell them he and Isabella were in love or that they had gotten married? Probably both.

"I've often wondered what he wanted to tell us." Unfortunately, they would never know the answer.

"How did he fall?" Caroline's voice cracked on the last word.

Don fisted his hand to keep from reaching for her.

Sorrow washed over Gantz's face. "He was leaning too far off the perch trying to take a shot. He lost his footing."

Caroline lowered her jaw. "You saw this?" Her tone sharpened. Good girl. Pride swelled in Don's chest. She was so much stronger than he was, able to harness her pain and work with it, not allow the past to hobble her. Unlike him.

Gantz looked startled by the question. Don's instincts reared.

"No. Actually, I was on the ground. Dennis and Randy had climbed up to take a look."

"So he could have been pushed for all you know…" Caroline mused.

Don bit the inside of his cheek to keep from smiling. She was leading the sheriff like a kitten with a laser light.

Gantz shook his head adamantly. "He wasn't. Randy and Dennis were best friends. Randy was devastated by Dennis's death."

Caroline asked, "What was Randy and Isabella's relationship like?"

"Friends. We all ran around together as kids."

"But what about when they were at college together?" Caroline pressed.

Gantz tilted his head, clearly not liking where this was headed. "What are you saying? Do you think Randy had a thing going with Isabella, too?"

"We don't know," Don contributed.

Gantz's demeanor turned from grieving friend to cop in a flash. "What *do* you know?"

Oops. But Don could play that game, too. He planted his feet, clasped his hands behind his back and squared up.

"Isabella was being stalked by someone who wanted to be with her, and wouldn't take no for an answer. She was pregnant and alone. Afraid to tell her parents what was going on, so she gave up her child because she didn't believe she could raise a baby on her own. And because she was afraid of what her stalker would do if he learned she was carrying another man's child. A month after giving birth she was murdered."

Don paused just long enough to see how the sheriff reacted to the one word any lawman should trip over regardless of the conversation's topic. Gantz didn't blink. *Okay.*

"The police labeled the crime a B and E. But the lead detective told Elijah there was no forced entry, which was withheld in the official police report. That detective passed away a decade ago, so there's no way of knowing why he left off that detail. Though I'd be willing to speculate he'd been paid off by the killer."

Gantz narrowed his gaze. "Who are you?"

Don could appreciate the older man's astuteness. He relaxed his stance and reached into his pocket for his identification. "I'm with Trent Associates, a protection specialist agency out of Boston."

Gantz inspected his credentials before handing them back. "Am I correct in assuming you believe the attempts on Ms. Tully's life have something to do with Isabella's death?"

"I'm not sure how everything fits together yet."

Every time they upturned a stone they uncovered more confusion.

"But one thing is for certain. There's a madman loose in your jurisdiction, Sheriff. One who has set his sights on Caroline."

And Don would risk everything to keep her safe.

"Yes, Randall Paladin is my brother," Abigail said. She sat on the sofa in the parlor, a home-decorating magazine lay open on the coffee table. Her children were nowhere to be seen.

Don hitched a hip on the arm of the winged-back chair that Caroline sat in. He watched Abigail closely. Her green eyes appeared a tad too bright. Panic? Or anger?

"Why did you keep it a secret?" Caroline asked.

Abigail arched a perfectly plucked eyebrow. "A secret? What are you talking about? Everyone around here knows we're related. Just because I didn't tell you, doesn't mean I was keeping my relationship to Randall a secret."

"Are you and your brother close?" Don asked.

"No. He didn't approve of my marriage to Samuel."

"Really? Why not?" Caroline asked.

The disbelief in her voice mirrored the same surprise rocketing through Don. Samuel Maddox had to have been considered a catch around these parts.

Abigail sighed. "My brother is all about everyone staying within their social class."

A convenient reoccurring theme. First Elijah, now Paladin. Yet Paladin was the Maddox family lawyer. A very valuable client to have in a generally lower income, struggling part of the country. Why would he disapprove of having a closer connection to the family? The discrepancy didn't add up.

"But you all played together as kids," Caroline said. "Surely any social barriers were dismantled long ago."

Abigail's mouth stretched in a stiff smile. "Playing as children is a far cry from marrying into the family. My father worked for Elijah. Randall still works for Elijah. My marrying into the Maddox family was a breach in etiquette." She all but sniffed in disdain for Caroline and Don's lack of understanding of the intricacies of Southern high society.

Don asked, "What was Randall's relationship with Isabella?"

Disapproval shifted in Abigail's gaze. "I don't wish to speak ill of the dead."

Caroline stiffened. "Excuse me?"

"Isabella had a wild streak." Abigail lowered her voice as if afraid someone would hear. "She had a baby out of wedlock. Need I say more?"

Caroline clenched her jaw so tight Don was sure she'd have an ache later. He was proud of her for not lashing out at her aunt for the unkind words.

Wanting to know what this woman knew of Isabella's life, Don asked, "Do you know who Isabella was involved with before she was murdered?"

"I heard rumors but I don't take stock in gossip."

"Except when you're doing the gossiping," Caroline muttered.

Before Don succumbed to a smile, he asked, "What were the rumors?"

"She and Georgie-Porgie had a fling before she left for college."

Don frowned and clarified, "George Gantz?"

Abigail waved a bejeweled hand. "Yes, our esteemed sheriff."

Curious that the sheriff never mentioned his feelings for Isabella. Don hadn't picked up on the deceit. The sheriff obviously had a good poker face. Or was Abigail lying?

"But as I said, it was only a rumor. I don't know if it's true." Abigail glanced coyly at Don. "But I do know George had a thing for Isabella." Her mouth twisted. "But then again, half the boys in Jefferson County had a thing for her. Like I said, wild."

"Including your brother?" Caroline's voice dripped with anger.

Abigail shrugged, the gesture so similar to that of her kids, Don was almost too distracted to see the flash of aversion cross her face.

"My brother wasn't immune to Isabella's charms any more than the other males in town. But Randall knew his place and he certainly wasn't chasing after Isabella."

Don figured she thought if she kept saying it, it would be true. Probably not so much.

Caroline's complexion had paled to a sickly hue. "How about Dennis Finch?"

Pursing her lips in thought, Abigail tilted her head. "I hardly think so. He joined the army right out of high school."

"You didn't see him when he returned?"

She shook her head. "No, I can't say that I did. But I was off at college myself by then."

"Where did you go?"

"Ole Miss, of course."

The University of Mississippi. Easy enough to verify—and probably true, at that. It was clear Abigail had set her sights on Samuel early on. It stood to reason she'd follow him to college. Something wasn't adding up, though. If Sheriff Gantz had had a relationship with Isabella, why hide it? Unless he was the man who had stalked her.

But why then come after Caroline?

Was there more than one murderer on the loose?

Later that evening, Caroline and Don retreated to the library. Don sat at the desk using Samuel's dial-up computer, while she curled up in a chair by the window trying to relax with a book. But after reading the same passage for the fifth time, she gave up. Drizzling rain marred the outside of the window pane and obscured the view of the surrounding woods, making her feel cut off from the rest of the world.

Letting her gaze stray across the room, she couldn't help watching Don. And enjoying the sight of his good looks. His fingers flew over the keyboard, his expression a study in intense concentration that added to his handsomeness.

She tried not to think about what it would be like after all this was over to not have Don around 24/7. She really dreaded going back to her former existence. Alone and lonely.

By choice, she reminded herself.

After Cullen's death and then discovering his betrayal, she'd kept herself isolated on purpose to protect herself from further pain. How could she ever trust someone so implicitly again?

Don wasn't anything like Cullen, her mind rationalized.

Yet, there were similarities. Both were charming, compassionate and smart.

But there was something about Don that drew her to him in a way she'd never felt before. His honor and integrity were real. Admitting to his post-traumatic stress disorder had to have been hard for a man who liked to be in control. Yet he wasn't afraid to be vulnerable with her. Knowing that he trusted her with his inner wounds made her feel special. He hadn't had to open up to her, that wasn't in his job description.

Don's gaze lifted from the laptop and collided with hers. Heat flushed through her face for being caught staring but she didn't look away. She wasn't going to reveal her thoughts, however. Now was not the time.

She did her best to pretend she'd simply been admiring his haircut and smiled. "What are you working on?"

One eyebrow twitched, but only slightly. "A little research into Sheriff Gantz. He was at the police academy in Jackson when Isabella was murdered."

"That's good, right?" She hated the idea of the sheriff being a murderer.

"I've confirmed it's an airtight alibi. But we still don't know what really happened when Dennis died. I had one of the investigators at Trent dig up Dennis's autopsy report. His injuries were consistent with a fall."

"An accident." Better than having both her biological parents murdered. But still awful. Horrifying.

"Maybe. A push wouldn't show up in autopsy, though. I'd like to hear Paladin's version to see if it lines up with Gantz's."

A blast of noise split the air and rattled the house all the way to the foundation. The lights flickered. Books fell from the wall, the sharp edges digging into her back. Stunned she jumped from the chair.

"Get down!" Don dove away from the desk and belly crawled to her side. "Come on!" he urged and pushed her toward the door.

Black smoke curled through the archway. The stench of burning wood assaulted her senses.

In the entryway, Abigail ushered her children out the door. Don and Caroline followed them out into the drizzling rain. Samuel ran from the side of the house to where they gathered on the driveway. Horace grabbed the hose and dragged it back around to the side of the house.

"The generator blew up," Samuel explained and coughed into his sleeve. He hugged his wife and children.

"We have to help put out the fire in the cellar!" The family was about to lose everything they had. Caroline moved, intending to run to aid Horace, but Don caught her about the waist.

"You stay here."

"The house!"

"I'll go." Don took off at a run, disappearing around the side of the house. Samuel quickly followed.

Caroline looked around. "Where's Mary?"

"I didn't see her," Abigail said.

"She was in the kitchen." Lilly began to cry.

Caroline's stomach tumbled. Mary could be hurt. "I'm going to go find her."

"Wait! It's not safe," Abigail called out.

Caroline couldn't let her grandmother die. She raced back inside.

TWELVE

Flames licked at the cellar doors. Burning wood crackled. Smoke thickened. Anxiety chomped through Don. He sprayed the fire extinguisher. His heart hammered in his chest. His breathing came out in ragged gasps. Vivid nightmares of the bombing that scarred his hand hovered at the periphery of his mind. He forced his concentration on the task at hand.

Beside him, Horace continued to douse the side of the house with a calmness Don envied. Samuel held the satellite phone in one hand and, with the other, helped to keep the hose from tangling in the bushes butting up against the outer wall.

"Fire department's on their way," Samuel called out.

"Samuel! Don!" Abigail and the twins skidded to a halt a few feet away.

One glance at the group and Don's stomach dropped. Fear sparked like the business end of a Taser. "Where's Caroline?"

"She went back in to find Mary," Landon said, his voice quivering.

"I tried to stop her," wailed Abigail.

Terror shot through Don's system. She was in danger.

If anything happened to her… His heart pitched. He couldn't lose her. Not like this. She'd become the most important person in his life. That realization spiraled through him, scaring him almost as much as the fire.

"My wife!" Horace ran toward the front door. Another explosion rocked the house and blew out the first-floor windows.

Don grabbed the older man and held him back. "You stay. I'll get them."

He stormed back through the front door. "Caroline!"

"Here!" Her faint cry came from the kitchen.

He raced down the hallway. Billowing clouds of smoke stung his eyes. The back wall of the house burned in a searing hot display of color. He found Caroline huddled over an unconscious Mary on the floor in the corner.

Tears streaked a sooty trail down Caroline's face. "Help her."

He easily lifted Mary into his arms. "Stay with me," he said to Caroline.

Swallowing the fear rising to choke him, he led her back the way they'd come through the dense black smoke. He could barely see the open front door. The sound of sirens drawing closer filled him with relief. Just a few more feet.

"Please, God, please let me get them out of here safely," he whispered. And hoped his prayer would be answered.

Behind him a door hinge creaked. A scuffle.

Caroline's choked scream stopped him in his tracks.

Shifting Mary in his arms to gain a more secure hold, he spun around. "Caroline!"

The hall was empty. She was gone.

Panic clogged his throat.

Fear clawed at him, leaving raw wounds. He had to get Mary out. Then he'd come back to find Caroline. She had to be here somewhere.

Forcing his feet forward, he stumbled out the door, depositing Mary into Horace's waiting arms. Fire trucks roared up the drive. Don couldn't wait for the firemen to rescue Caroline. He had to save her. He couldn't fail her. She'd trusted him to protect her.

He ran back inside. Visibility was zero. He listened intently, but heard only the roar of the fire, the groaning of the house protesting the assault.

"Caroline!"

No answer.

His gaze searched the entryway, the hall. She'd been right behind him....

Where could she be?

"Dear Lord, help!" Don cried.

A strong hand clamped over Caroline's mouth. The barrel of a handgun dug painfully into her ribs.

"Move!"

The harsh masculine command echoed in her head. There was something vaguely familiar about the voice, but her overwhelmed senses couldn't latch onto where she'd heard it before.

"Down the stairs."

Darkness was disorienting. She stumbled down the steps, missing the last stair and landing at the bottom on her hands and knees. She felt an earthen floor. Cool air touched her skin.

The man jerked her to her feet, his hand still in place over her mouth, the gun now at her kidney. "Walk!"

The fire's toxic fumes didn't penetrate the tunnel she was being forced to move through. She breathed through her nose. The musky smell of dirt filled her nostrils.

Elijah had been right. There were secret passageways in the house. She'd been following Don when someone grabbed her from behind and dragged her into what she thought was a closet, but actually was the opening to a tunnel. Faintly, she heard Don yelling her name. He must be out of his mind with worry. She knew how important protecting her was to him. Would he think to look in the closet? Would she ever see him again?

Please, God, let him find me before it's too late.

She had to do something to alert him. Something to save herself. She cocked her elbow and then swung her arm back, using her elbow like a hammer, delivering a hard blow to her captive's chest.

"Oof!" His hold over her mouth slipped.

She took advantage and sank her teeth in his flesh.

He yanked his hand away with a curse.

Immediately, she let loose as loud a scream as her oxygen-deprived lungs could muster as she tried to push past the man. He caught his balance and punched her hard in her stomach. She doubled over with a swoosh as the air left her body in a pain-filled exhale.

"Your boyfriend won't hear you," the man mocked and shoved her forward. "Keep moving."

Her hands groped the slimy moss-covered sides of the tunnel. Loose dirt tumbled through her fingers. They were far beneath the house. She stumbled on the uneven floor. "Where are you taking me?"

"Shut up!"

Another hard shove sent her lurching forward.

Hopelessness threatened to bring her to her knees. Was this dank blackness going to be her coffin?

Remembering the squeak of a hinge, Don flung open the nearest closet door. He struggled to pull in a breath. Through the thickening smoke he saw hanging coats pushed to one side exposing the back wall. A sooty handprint marred the white paint.

Pulse racing, he stepped into the closet and pushed at the wall. It swung open, revealing a dark hole. Without hesitation, he stepped through. His foot hit the edge of a stair, then air. He went tumbling down, bouncing over the crude stairs, feeling the dig of pain with each bump. He curled, protecting his neck until he landed in a heap at the bottom, the air knocked out of his lungs.

He lay in the pitch-blackness, orienting himself.

None of his nightmares came even close to the suffocating panic rising to choke him.

A woman screamed.

Caroline!

Pulling himself together, he rose and ran toward the sound, toward the woman he loved.

He loved her.

The thought reverberated through him, stretching his already strung out nerves to the point of breaking. He had to find her. Help her. Save her.

If he let her down, he didn't know what he would do. Or how he would survive knowing he'd failed at the most important moment of his life.

Several agonizing minutes later, Caroline rammed up against a wall. "Ouch!" She rubbed her nose.

The man reached around her. The wall slid back.

Light invaded the tunnel revealing another flight of stairs.

"Up!" the man barked. "Don't try anything funny or I'll shoot you."

Scrambling up the steps, she could only hope escape awaited at the top. She wanted to see Don again. She wanted him to hold her and make the big, bad world go away. With him she'd be safe.

The staircase led to the interior of a shed filled with wood workbenches, cluttered with rusted tools. A bright yellow riding lawn mower occupied the space in the center and an overflowing can of empty, glass wine and beer bottles sat in the corner. Possible weapons, if she could only get to one.

Caroline knew where they were. The ramshackle outbuilding on the other side of the detached garage. In the distance she heard the commotion of the firefighters working to control the flames engulfing the main house.

She sent up a silent plea, *Please let Don have gotten out in time!*

Assessing her surroundings, she gauged the shed to be about five by eight. A set of double doors behind the mower gave her hope. An escape route.

"Don't even think about it!"

She twisted to look at the man climbing out of the stairwell behind her, holding a gun aimed at her chest.

Paladin.

Confusion whirled in her mind. "Why are you doing this?"

He shoved her away from him. "You're an abomination. You should never have been born."

"I don't understand," Caroline said. "You're Aunt Abigail's brother. You're family."

His lips twisted in a sinister grimace. "I'm not family. I should have been. But no, Isabella thought she was too good for me. Me!"

Of course! The pieces of the puzzle fell into place. "You loved my mother. You were the man she talked about in her diary who wouldn't leave her alone. The man she was afraid of."

His lip curled at the corner. "If she'd only listened to reason. I would have been good for her."

She needed to keep him talking and distracted while she inched her way closer to freedom, she said, "But she didn't love you. She loved Dennis."

Hatred spiked his gray eyes, making them appear to shine. "That's right. She married the son of the hired help." He snorted in derision. "It was insulting."

"Is that why you claimed to disapprove of Abigail's marriage to Samuel?"

"Yes! It wasn't fair. I should have been the one to be accepted into the Maddox clan, not her."

Swallowing back the rising tide of bile, she stared, seeing the madness in his gaze. "The day of Dennis's death. You were with him. He told you about the elopement and you pushed him from the hunting perch."

"No one can prove that."

Heartsick, she asked, "Does Abigail know? Does she know you killed Dennis and my mother?"

He gave a short bark of dry laughter. "Abigail. Miss High and Mighty. Nabbed the wealthy Samuel Maddox. Rubs my nose in it, she does. She was good enough for a Maddox, but I wasn't."

"So you *did* kill them both." Caroline inched closer

to the mower. If she could get on the other side of the large piece of machinery, she could use it as cover if he started shooting. Her foot rolled on a loose piece of pipe.

Carefully, scooting the pipe behind her with her toe, she asked, "So why did you switch Elijah's pills?"

"Pills? What are you talking about?" He sounded truly puzzled. He waved the gun. "Stop moving."

She took another step back. Either he would shoot, or he wouldn't. "But why come after me? What have I done to you?"

A vein began to bulge on his forehead as his aggravation increased. "You're a reminder."

Caroline shuddered. Clearly the man had issues. "Were you the one who tried to strangle me in my room?"

He snorted. "Yes. You're stronger than you look."

And hopefully smarter. "And the tree? Did you set off the charge that brought it down?"

His mouth curved. "I did." Pride infused in his voice. "I needed some way to keep everyone distracted while I hid and waited for the right moment to strike."

Her stomach roiled as she inched farther away, moving the pipe on the floor with her foot. "How did you find the passageway under the house?"

"We found it when we were kids."

"We?"

"Isabella, Dennis and me." He cackled. "It was our secret."

She bumped up against the nose of the riding mower. She watched Paladin's eyes flare as he realized what she was about to do. A bullet slammed into the mower's engine. She dived behind the mower, her hand quickly palming the pipe and crawled toward the door.

Paladin was on her fast, his hand fisting in her hair. He jerked her to her feet. She came up swinging. The metal piece of pipe glanced off his shoulder. He grabbed her wrist before she could bring the pipe down on his head. He yanked her arm behind her so far she thought it would snap.

"You stupid girl, you're just like your mother. No one bests me."

He pushed her toward the mower. "Sit!"

Fear seared her senses. She twisted and lashed out with her fists, her blows landing with useless thuds. Unfazed, he roughly forced her to sit on the wide metal seat. From the pocket of his coat he brought out two white plastic zip ties.

Horrified, Caroline tried to bail off the mower in the opposite direction. He smacked her across the head with the gun. Pain exploded behind her eyes. The room spun. Her arms were jerked forward and bound to the mower's steering wheel. Next he secured her feet together. The plastic cut into her flesh.

She blinked to clear her vision. Focus, focus. Deep down inside she knew he was going to kill her. Murder her like he'd murdered Isabella and Dennis. Panic threatened to rob her of sanity. She filled her lungs and let out a bloodcurdling scream. Another vicious blow cut the scream off. He yanked a rag from a nearby workbench and stuffed the filthy material into her mouth. She gagged on the bitter taste of mechanical grease and turpentine on the rag.

He rummaged around until he found a can of gasoline. The grin spreading across his face sent terror sliding over her. "Too easy."

He unscrewed the cap and doused the workbench and walls with the accelerant. He took out a matchbook from his breast pocket. "By the time they all realize there's another fire, you'll be a crispy critter."

With a glee-filled laugh, he lit a match and flipped it toward the workbench.

The horrifying rumble of the gasoline igniting filled her ears. Beyond terrified, Caroline watched the growing blaze consume the shed. She tried to wrench her hands free, her feet. She couldn't move. Tears stung her eyes. Scorching heat blasted her in the face. She was going to burn to death. An image of Don seared her brain. His beloved face, those mesmerizing eyes. She'd never see him again. Never be able to tell him—

Paladin leaned in close cutting off her thoughts. "Say hello to your mother."

Then he disappeared out the double doors and into the night. She heard the sound of a motor turn over. The glare of headlights swept past the opened doors as he roared away. She was alone.

Please, Lord, her mind screamed as she yanked against the binds holding her in place. *Please don't let me die like this.*

Again she prayed that Don would find her in time. That she'd have the chance to tell him she loved him.

But how would he know where to search?

Don reached the dead end of the tunnel. "No!"

Fear sliced deep gouges through him. He pounded his fist against the wooden wall. He forced himself to breathe. There had to be a way to open this panel. He pushed at the wall. It didn't budge.

Trying to remain calm and in control of the raging terror strangling him, he ran his hands over the edges until he felt an anomaly in the highest corner. A small lever. Using his fingers, he depressed the lever. The wall slid open to reveal another staircase. Bright light chased away the dark. He flinched, his eyes adjusting. The strong smell of gasoline assaulted him. The sizzle of a blaze raised the hairs at the back of his neck.

Caroline.

He rushed up the stairs. The sight that met his eyes stole his breath.

Caroline was secured to a lawn mower. Her head lolled to the side, her eyes were closed. He had to reach her before the fire caused the gas in the mower's tank to explode.

"Please, God, don't let her die. Please answer me with a yes this one time!"

He rushed forward. The walls began to crumble around them. Cinders burned through his shirt but he barely noticed the sting. A pair of garden shears hung on a hook by the door. He yanked them down and snipped the ties binding Caroline to the mower. He scooped her up in his arms and ran out the double doors.

Dropping to his knees a safe distance away from the burning shed, he laid her carefully on the soft, wet ground. He placed two fingers on the artery in her neck. She had a pulse. "Thank You, God."

But she wasn't breathing.

A fresh wave of alarm broke over him. He tilted her head back, pinched her nose, closed his mouth over hers and exhaled. When the air was expelled from his lungs, he lifted his head to draw in a big breath and repeated the process, filling her with oxygen.

She coughed. Relief infused him, washing away the tension in his chest. He gathered her close, love for this incredible woman overflowing within his heart. She'd endured so much.

"Caroline, talk to me," Don urged, stroking back a lock of hair from her beautiful face. Using his thumb, he wiped black soot from the fire away from her cheek.

Her eyelids fluttered open. Fear flared. She let out a gasp.

"Shh, you're safe." Don drew her closer.

She struggled to sit up. "Paladin. He's getting away. He killed Isabella and Dennis."

Sheriff Gantz crouched beside them. "He won't get far."

Suddenly they were surrounded. Firemen in turnout gear worked to put out the burning shed.

The Maddox family crowded around them. Concern and fear was etched on their faces.

"What happened?" Samuel asked, alarm ringing in his tone.

Abigail wiped at her tears. "Is she okay?"

The twins huddled close to their parents.

"The paramedics are waiting." Gantz gestured to the two uniformed men hovering nearby with their gear.

Don acknowledged them with a nod. "Let the paramedics take care of you."

He tried to hand her over, but her hands fisted in his shirt, keeping him from moving.

"You're here," she said with awe in her voice. "I

prayed you'd come." She snuggled closer, laying her head against his heart. "I love you."

Her words seared through him more painfully than any fire possibly could. He loved her, too. Loved her enough to know that he had to let her go. For her sake. He couldn't take the risk that he'd ever hurt her, disappoint her. She'd had enough of that in her life. Tears burned the back of his eyes but he forced them back.

The Rules of Protection were in place for a reason. If he stayed true to the tenets he'd lived by his adult life, then he couldn't hurt or disappoint anyone.

Hardening his heart against the ache of loss that scored him to the core, he staggered to his feet and carried Caroline to the waiting ambulance bay. The paramedics took over, placing her on the gurney and hoisted her into the back of the vehicle. Don climbed in beside her.

He job wasn't finished until Paladin was captured.

She clutched his hand, her gaze searching his face. "Don?"

"Everything will be fine," he assured her.

Though he knew he'd never be fine again. Not without her.

"Randall is behind bars," Sheriff Gantz announced as he entered Caroline's hospital room.

Caroline let out a sigh of relief. The threat to her life was over. She no longer had to fear that someone wanted her dead.

"Where did you find him?" Don rose from the chair he'd been occupying for the past twelve hours while she recovered from smoke inhalation.

Her injuries could have been so much worse. She

could have been burned, but she knew deep in her soul God had put a hedge of protection around her, keeping the fire at bay until Don arrived. Her hero. Love flooded through her. She vaguely remembered telling him of her feelings, but the memory was jumbled. Had she only thought the words, or had she said them out loud?

Needing to feel connected to him, she reached for his hand.

He slipped his hand over hers, the warmth of his skin sending tingles up her arm. He had to have feelings for her too, right?

"Nabbed him at the airport. He had a one-way ticket to France. Cashed out his bank accounts and intended to disappear," the sheriff said. "He made a full confession to the murders of Isabella and Dennis, and the attempts on Caroline's life."

Don narrowed his gaze. "And what of Elijah and the pills?"

Gantz shook his head. "Denies any involvement in that."

"He said the same to me," Caroline stated, remembering Paladin's puzzlement when she brought up the subject.

"However, we do have a suspect in custody in the attempt to poison Mr. Maddox."

"Who?" Caroline asked.

"Abigail Maddox," Don supplied without any surprise.

Caroline gasped.

"That's correct," Gantz confirmed. "We traced the purchase of the salt tablets to her."

Stunned, Caroline tried to make sense of it. "Why would she do that?"

"Apparently she's been pressuring Samuel to move away, but he won't leave while Elijah is still alive," Gantz supplied.

Don squeezed her hand. "When Elijah became ill she saw an opportunity to hurry his death along."

Sympathy filled Caroline. "Poor Uncle Samuel. And the twins!" Her heart ached to think they'd have to endure their mother going to prison.

"Don't feel too bad for them. They admitted to setting the smoke bomb and putting the snake in your bed," Gantz said. "They both claim their mother put them up to it."

"But you don't believe them?" Don asked.

He shrugged. "She may have made the suggestion, but they're old enough to know right from wrong. Samuel has hired a team of lawyers for his family."

Exhausted, emotionally and physically, Caroline closed her eyes. "It's all so sad and sordid."

"Knock, knock," a familiar voice called from the doorway.

Caroline's eyelids popped open. She squealed in delight to see Elijah enter in a wheelchair pushed by an orderly. "Elijah!"

Elijah's face split into a beaming smile. He looked vibrant and healthier than she could have imagined. "Caroline. I've been so worried."

Don made space for Elijah so he could be wheeled to her bedside.

"I'll leave you now," Sheriff Gantz said, heading toward the door. He stopped to say to Elijah, "Good to see you, Elijah."

"And you, George," Elijah said, shaking the sheriff's hand. "Thank you for all you've done."

"Doing my job, sir. Don, a word?"

Don nodded and glanced at Caroline, "I'll be right outside."

Her heart smiled. He was still protecting her. She watched him disappear out the door. She let out a small sigh.

"He's something, this fiancé of yours," Elijah stated, drawing her attention. "I approve wholeheartedly."

The need to confess the truth bubbled to the surface. "He's actually not my fiancé." *Yet*. The word hovered on her tongue. "He's a bodyguard I hired to accompany me here. We were pretending to be engaged to cover his true purpose for coming with me."

Elijah's hazel eyes widened. "A bodyguard? Well, doesn't that beat all? I never would have guessed. You two seemed so much in love." He peered at her speculatively. "Are you sure your feelings for each other were all pretend?"

She grinned at her too-observant grandfather. "No, I'm not sure at all."

Elijah grinned back. "You do love him."

Heat rose up her neck. "Yes, I do."

"Have you told him?"

"Not properly yet, but I plan to."

Elijah patted her hand. "Good to hear. And if I were a betting man, which I'm not mind you, I'd bet Don loves you, too."

"I sure hope so."

"Well, we both made it to the New Year."

"Yes, we did. Happy New Year, Elijah."

"Grandfather," he corrected. "Happy New Year to

you, my dear." His happy expression dimmed. "I suppose you'll be heading back to Boston soon."

She squeezed his hand. "Yes. But I'll come to visit often."

"I'll hold you to that promise."

Don stepped back into the room. "Samuel is here to see you both."

Caroline exchanged a glance with Elijah. They smiled simultaneously. "Invite him in," she said.

Samuel walked in, carrying a bouquet of brightly colored tulips and carnations. His tentative expression tugged at her heart. "Uncle Samuel, are you okay?"

"I should be asking you that," he said, laying the flowers on the edge of the bed. "Father, I'm so sorry."

Elijah held out his free hand to his son. "Not your doing, son. The house?"

Samuel shook his head. "Unsalvageable."

Sadness damped Elijah's gaze. "We can rebuild. And the twins?"

"Confused, angry and scared. But they'll survive."

Samuel ran a hand over his jaws. "I'm having a hard time reconciling Abigail's actions with the woman I love. But I guess we're all capable of a dark side."

Caroline had come face-to-face with darkness in that shed. She hoped she never had to go through something like that again. Her gaze went to Don. As long as he was in her life, she'd never have to face anything alone.

Now if they could only have a private moment so she could ask him if he'd be willing to spend the rest of his life with her.

She stifled a giggle. She wanted to propose to Don. What a wonderful way to start the New Year.

THIRTEEN

Much to Caroline's annoyance and frustration the moment she'd been hoping for didn't arrive until she and Don were back in Boston. Don's reticent mood on the trip home left her feeling off-kilter. Though there wasn't any concrete reason she could pinpoint, he seemed to be pulling away from her. The job he'd been hired to do was done. She understood that. But there were still words unsaid, feelings needing to be explored. Nervous anticipation knotted her stomach.

After the taxi from Logan Airport dropped them off in front of her apartment building, she waited on the sidewalk with her bags while Don stowed his own bags in the back of his Porsche that he'd left parked on the street. A recent storm had covered the city with a pristine blanket of snow. She shivered and pulled her wool coat tighter. She couldn't believe she actually missed Mississippi's milder rainy weather.

She led the way to her apartment, while Don carried her bags. The awkward silence charged the air between them. Once inside she flipped up the heat.

Don set her bags inside the doorway, but remained in the hall. "I'll say goodbye here."

"Wait! No." An anxious flutter hit her tummy. Taking a bracing breath, she said, "Please come in."

He shook his head. "I need to get to the office and write up my report."

"Surely you can spare a moment." She cleared her throat. "I've something to ask you."

Stepping inside, he closed the door behind him.

"Would you like some tea, a glass of water?" she asked using the courtesy as a stalling tactic.

He shook his head, his teal-blue eyes studying her. "What's wrong, Caroline?"

A nervous laugh escaped. "Wrong? Thankfully nothing anymore." She gestured to the new door. "The super did a super job on replacing my door." An embarrassed laugh escaped for her word play.

His mouth twitched. "You had something you wanted to ask?"

She bit at her lip. Her courage faltered. She gestured toward the leather couch. "Yes, I do have something to ask. Can we sit?"

With a slight frown he moved to the couch. She sat next to him. "I can't thank you enough for all you've done for me these past weeks."

"No thanks needed. I was doing what you hired me to do."

"I know that." She frowned. Why was he acting so strange, so distant? His expression gave nothing away of his thoughts. "But we've grown close, right? I'm more than just a job to you, aren't I?"

"Caroline—"

She didn't like the tone in his voice.

Gathering her bravery, she looked him square in the eye. "I'm in love with you."

He inhaled sharply.

He sat immobile, his face etched like a perfect piece of granite. Hard and intractable. Not the reaction she'd expected.

"I'm sure you think you are," he said finally. "We shared an intense time. You were almost killed. Your emotions are running high. Give yourself some time to settle back into your life here. You'll see that you don't really…that your feelings aren't what you think they are. It's not uncommon for protectees to develop feelings for their protector."

Her hackles rose even as hurt gored her on a spike of disbelief. "I know what I feel. I love you, Don."

Shaking his head, he said, "We can't do this. *I* can't do this."

Taken aback by the alarm in his eyes, she said, "Don, I don't understand. Are you telling me you don't feel anything for me?" She braced herself for his answer, realizing in a flash of clarity that he'd never indicated any deep feelings for her. Sure he held her hand, hugged, kissed her even. But he'd never uttered any promises or declarations. Tears welled in her eyes.

He rose to his feet and stalked a path in front of her. "Caroline, you're wonderful, kind, compassionate. I would give my life for you."

"You almost did, several times." She took heart in the fact that he hadn't denied having any feelings for her outright. All the emotions of affection and caring she'd been feeling couldn't have been one-sided. Could they? "I don't understand what the problem is. Either you care for me or you don't."

"It's not that simple. You've been through enough hurt and pain in your life, I won't risk adding to it."

Confusion seeped through her. "You would never hurt me."

"Not intentionally, no. But—"

Her heart beat in her throat. "But?"

He stopped short and faced her. His hands fisted at his sides. Agony marched across his face. She wanted to go to him but feared he'd reject her. She sat still—waiting, knowing that whatever he was about to say was going to hurt.

"I'm afraid I'll be like my father. A loser who cracks under the pressure and responsibility of a family. And I couldn't face you never forgiving me."

Boggled by his words, she stood. "You are not your father. You could never be like him."

When he opened his mouth to argue, she held up a hand. "I don't know what twisted logic brought you to this conclusion, but look at the life choices you've made. The military? Talk about pressure and responsibility. Caring for your dying mother? Protecting people you don't know? These aren't actions of someone who would ever crack under pressure."

"But there's no guarantee," he said in a voice so full of pain and resignation.

"Don't you think I know that?" Her fists clenched. All her rage at the unfairness of her past relationship screamed through her. "I'm not the naive girl I once was. I know that life can turn on a dime, feelings ebb and flow, but I believe in my gut that you and I would not be a statistic. You and I together would be good. We have God on our side." She reached out for him. "He's the only guarantee I need. His grace will protect us."

"I wish I could believe that." He walked away, out of her reach. "I'm sorry, Caroline."

With his back ramrod straight and his expression hard and full of pain, he left her apartment, closing the door softly behind him.

Caroline stood frozen in place, barely believing he was gone. Then slowly she sank to her knees and burst into tears.

Don couldn't concentrate. It had been two days since he'd walked out of Caroline's life. Two days of going through the motions, not really feeling anything, afraid to allow the pain in for fear he'd end up crippled by it.

This morning, as he sat at his desk, the buzz of the other agents doing their work all around him retreated to white noise. The images of Caroline's hurt-filled eyes, the way she'd looked when he'd left her standing in her living room, wouldn't be denied. They bore into him like a laser, pinpointing the soft, tender place where she'd taken up residence in his heart.

His soul ached knowing the pain he'd caused her. Exactly what he'd been trying to avoid. He couldn't win. Not telling her how he felt hurt her. But wouldn't being with her lead to pain, too?

We have God on our side. He's the only guarantee I need.

Her words, spoken with such conviction, rang inside his head. It sounded so simple, trust God with their lives.

A pair of fingers snapped in front of his face. "Dude, snap out of it."

His gaze shifted to Kyle.

Kyle arched an eyebrow. "Man, ever since your return from M-I-S-S-I-S-S-I-P-P-I—" he said each letter in a singsong voice that grated down Don's back

"—your head hasn't been in the game." Kyle tapped his knuckles on the dossier lying open in front of Don.

Blowing out a breath, Don nodded. "Gotcha."

But he couldn't work up the wherewithal to present a plan of action for this newest case. He was doing his fellow employees a disservice. As well as the client. Gathering the file, he held it out to Kyle. "I need to talk to Trent."

Kyle accepted the folder with surprise.

Don made his way upstairs and knocked on James's office door.

"Come in."

Don entered. James stood at the picture window, his feet braced apart, his hands clasped behind his back. He turned to face Don. "I've been expecting you."

Don blinked. *Okay.* "Why?"

"A package arrived for you." He gestured with his head to toward the desk.

Don cautiously approached and inspected the airmail package. The label read Sheriff Gantz. Don's gut clenched. He knew what was inside. "Sir, I need to request some vacation time."

Approval shone bright on James's face. "Good. Some time away will help you take a long look at what you want in life."

Don's eyebrows rose. The uncanny way James knew when his team members needed space had always been a source of conversation among the staff. Being so easily read made Don feel vulnerable and yet known and cared for all at the same time.

"I trust you'll find what you're searching for soon. I'd hate to lose you," James continued.

"I'll be back, sir," Don assured him.

James nodded sagely and resumed contemplating the scenery out his window.

Don liked working for Trent. Liked protecting others.

These aren't the actions of someone who would ever crack under pressure.

Something inside of him shifted. Did he dare believe that? His breath caught and held. His parents hadn't trusted their lives to God. If they had, would his father have left? Maybe cracking under pressure wasn't a part of Don's DNA. With God anything was possible. Right? An excitement he hadn't ever felt before stirred in his soul.

As he pulled the door closed, James called over his shoulder, "Tell Ms. Tully hello, will you?"

Don dropped his chin forward. How *did* he do that?

Don left the agency and took his Porsche for a drive. His baby handled the curves with ease, allowing his troubled mind to examine his wants and desires.

Take a long look at what you want in life.

Being honest with himself, Don acknowledged he didn't want to grow old alone and lonely, wishing he'd seized the opportunity for love when he had the chance.

Fear, he decided, was a horrible companion.

The only antidote to fear was love. God's love. Caroline's love.

"Lord, I pray it's not too late. I love her." Joy expanded in his chest, crowding out the last vestiges of fear.

And he needed to tell her.

He pulled to the side of the road and reached for his cell phone. Scrolling through his contacts, he found her number. Figuring she'd be at the store since it was the afternoon, he dialed that number first. A woman answered.

"Caroline Tully, please?"

"I'm sorry, she's unavailable. Would you like to leave a message?"

"This is Donovan Cavanagh, could you please have her return my call?"

There was a moment's hesitation, and then the woman said, "I know who you are. She's visiting her parents in New Hampshire. Would you like that number?"

"I have it, thank you." Don hung up and then started to dial Caroline's parents' number. He stopped. Telling her he loved her couldn't be done properly over the phone. She'd had the courage to face him when she declared her love. He could do no less. He hoped showing up on her parents' doorstep wouldn't upset her. Only one way to find out.

With hopes high, he headed to New Hampshire.

With one gloved hand, Caroline brushed away the snow from the bronze memorial plate embedded in the ground at the head of Cullen's grave. Her other hand crushed the stems of the small bouquet of posies she'd brought. She blew out a breath. So many emotions swirled in her heart and head. She tried to grab ahold of one long enough to examine, but they floated away like the powdery snow blowing off the tall dogwoods surrounding the cemetery.

"So much has happened this month," she said aloud. Then gave a soft laugh. "I fell in love again. Only he doesn't love me. At least not enough to take a chance on us."

What was she doing here? She hadn't been back since the funeral. Too much anger and bitterness had kept her away.

You haven't forgiven him.

Don's statement twirled around her mind.

It struck her then why she'd felt compelled to come here today. She longed for peace.

And closure.

Like the closure she'd had with Don. He'd explained his position and even though she didn't understand or agree with his reasons, she respected that he hadn't strung her along, given her false hope or illusions. She knew exactly where he stood.

You haven't forgiven him.

Self-knowledge was a powerful thing. She could see now that the unforgiveness she'd been harboring had lain trapped in her soul like a festering cancer. Tainting her world.

I couldn't face you never forgiving me.

She made a strangled sound. Don's words hadn't registered at the time, but now she understood. Understood what she needed to do to find peace.

She laid the bundled flowers on the plaque.

"I forgive you, Cullen. I forgive you." With each utterance, she felt lighter, freer.

Peaceful.

If only her heart didn't ache with longing for Don.

She stood and dusted the snow off her pants. "Goodbye, Cullen."

Driving through the town of Wilton brought back memories of her childhood and teenage years. The ice cream shop on the corner, once her favorite hangout. Ms. Vandervelde's music's school where she'd taken piano lessons that hadn't stuck. The grade school looked tired and old.

When she pulled in to her parents' driveway, her heart skipped a beat.

Parked next to her father's pickup truck was a silver Porsche. Don's car.

What was he doing here?

Giddy anticipation gushed through her and she quickly tempered it down. She couldn't let her hopes soar. There had to be a logical, explainable reason he'd tracked her to her parents' home, something related to her case. She stepped on to the porch and her dad whipped open the door. The excited look on his face gave her pause.

"You have a visitor," he stated.

"I see that," she replied, giving him a curious once-over. "You okay, Dad?"

He grinned. "Never better."

She entered the living room to find her mother and Don in quiet conversation. Don lifted his gaze, his eyes caressed her and a smile teased the corners of his mouth. Her heart throbbed in her chest.

Her mother rose and hurried to her father's side. "We'll leave you two alone."

Bemused, Caroline watched her parents disappear into the kitchen.

Slowly she faced Don, the sight of him sweet torture. "Why are you here?"

He stood and walked to her. Taking her hand in his, he said, "To ask for your forgiveness."

She frowned. "You haven't done anything that needs forgiving."

The tender look in his eyes made her pulse pound. "I acted like a pigheaded chump."

A laugh relieved some tension. "Pigheaded, maybe. But never a chump."

"You're too generous." He drew her to the couch. "I was an idiot, too full of fear to see the gift right before me."

Her breath stalled. "Gift?"

"You offered me your heart, and I pushed you away." He brought her knuckles to his lips and gently kissed each one. "Can you forgive me?"

Despite her best effort, hope blossomed. "Yes. I forgive you." The forgiving wasn't closure, she hoped, but an opening to a wonderful future. A quiver of anticipation struck her. "You drove all the way here to ask for my forgiveness?"

"I also wanted to tell you, I love you."

Joy overflowed within her heart. "You don't know how much I wanted to hear you say that."

He slipped to one knee on the floor beside her and took her hands in his. Her eyes widened in delighted surprise.

"Will you marry me?"

She could hardly breathe.

Uncertainty flashed in his eyes. "Well, will you?"

Unable to speak, she nodded.

Pleasure lit up his face. "I'll buy you any ring you want."

She slipped to her knees and stared into his gorgeous eyes. "I don't need anything fancy as long as I have you."

He pulled her into a tight embrace. His lips captured hers, at once tender and searching, and oh, so welcome.

When they drew apart, he said, "Oh, I almost forgot." He picked up an airmail package sitting on the coffee table. "This is for you."

"A present?" She eagerly ripped into the envelope and slipped the contents out onto the table. She let out an elated cry. "Isabella's diary and yearbook. How did you get these?"

"The fire department managed to save them. Sheriff Gantz mailed them to me when he released all the evidence."

"I love you!" She threw her arms around Don's neck. "I'm so happy. I can't begin to tell you."

"You'll have the rest of our lives to tell me."

Planting her lips over his, she murmured, "Happy New Year."

EPILOGUE

Easter Sunday was a beautiful spring day in Mississippi. A day full of hope and peace. After the service,
Caroline walked down the center aisle of the Fayette
Community Church with Don by her side, their fingers
interlaced, and her Mississippi family not far behind.
She and Don had only arrived in town last night and
were staying at a bed-and-breakfast near one of the
properties Elijah owned, an apartment complex where
the family was living.

She exited the cool interior of the church and
emerged into sunshine and fresh air. Rays of sunlight
warmed her cheeks. A slight breeze kicked up the sweet
scent of the gardenia corsage pinned to the lapel of her
knee-length dress. A perfect day!

Don reached out to tuck a flyaway wisp of hair
behind her ear. "Glad we came?"

She nodded, love for this man surging through her
heart. "Definitely. Thank you."

He leaned in and brushed his lips across hers. "Anything for you."

She knew he meant the words. The past three months
had shown her that. This trip, too. He'd suggested they

fly down to personally invite her Mississippi family to their wedding, scheduled for September in New Hampshire.

She sighed with contentment and wished they were alone so she could wrap her arms around him and keep on kissing him. But they were in public, and they had their whole lives together to look forward to.

"The service was lovely," she commented to her grandfather as he and Samuel stopped beside her.

"I'm so happy you two were here to enjoy this with us," Elijah replied, his craggy face breaking into a grin. He looked amazingly well. His Addison's was under control and his doctor said Elijah could easily live to see another decade.

She sure hoped so.

"Cousin Caroline," Lilly called from the edge of the large manicured lawn adjacent to the white church building. She wore a sundress and had her dark hair pulled back into a low ponytail, making her look younger and so carefree. Much different from a few months before. "Come help us with the Easter egg hunt."

"Be right there," Caroline called back, happy to be included.

Lilly waved and ran to catch up to Landon, who led a group of kindergartners to the center of the lawn where Horace and Mary passed out small wicker baskets. Affection infused her, widening her smile. She and Mary had kept in touch over the past few months with weekly phone calls. Now that the family lived in town, they all had cell phones and computers and, much to the twins' delight, a television. Elijah had relaxed his stance on "no electronics" along with other things.

"Ah, to be that young again," Elijah said with a bit of wistfulness in his tone as he watched the festivities.

"I'm sure the kids would love your help, Dad," Samuel said.

Elijah chuckled. "I think you're right." He ambled away toward the revelry with a spring in his step.

Caroline turned to Samuel. "The twins seem in good spirits."

From the moment Caroline and Don had arrived back in Fayette to visit for the special weekend, the twins had been warm and welcoming. They now treated her like family. She enjoyed feeling so accepted, a way she hadn't felt at Christmastime.

Samuel sighed. "Yes, they are. They've been seeing a psychologist twice a week since…well, since Abigail went to prison."

The sadness in his eyes hurt Caroline's heart. She could only imagine how hard this situation must be for Samuel and the kids. Abigail would be in prison for at least three years before she'd be eligible for parole.

Hoping to convey her sympathy, Caroline laid a hand on her uncle's arm. "I'm sorry."

He patted her hand. "Not your fault, my dear. We'll get through this."

Don slipped his arm around her waist. She leaned into him, grateful that he always seemed to know just when she needed his support and strength.

"When we're done here, I'll take you out to see the progress on the house," Samuel said, clearly needing to change the subject.

"I'd like that," Caroline said. Elijah had explained that there'd been too much damage to the house's struc-ture—caused by the fire and the water from the fire hoses—to be repaired, so the building had been razed and they were rebuilding. Much as they were rebuilding their lives. She imagined great improvements for all of them come summertime. A fresh start. A new beginning. They all needed it.

"Cousin Caroline!" Lilly called again. "Come on. You're missing out!"

"I guess that's my cue," Caroline said. "Don?"

"Sure," he replied with a grin. "Wouldn't want to miss out on all the fun."

Slipping her hand into his, Caroline knew they'd never miss out on anything as long as they were together. She squeezed his hand. Together. She really liked the sound of that.

* * * * *

Dear Reader,

I hope you enjoyed the second installment of Protection Specialists. We first saw Donovan and Caroline as secondary characters in my November 2009 release *Chasing Shadows*. They'd had a spark then, so it seemed right to give them a story of their own. With Don's military background, he made for a great protector. Pair that with Caroline's gutsy spirit and need to know her past, and I had a two strong characters to work with.

The idea for the suspense part of the story came out of a childhood love for Nancy Drew mysteries. As a preteen, I wanted to grow up to be Nancy. I had the red hair! Plus, she always had a hunky admirer following her and her best friends around. What could be better? My favorite books were *The Hidden Staircase* and *The Secret in the Attic*. I can vividly remember sitting in the summer sun devouring my collection of Nancy Drew mysteries. I saved them all. My daughter has enjoyed them, and hopefully one day I'll have a granddaughter who will find herself swept away into many mysteries with Nancy and the gang.

Keep an eye out for more Protection Specialists stories coming soon. Until then, may God shine upon you with love and joy,

Questions for Discussion

1. What made you pick up this book to read? In what ways did it live up to your expectations?

2. In what ways were Don and Caroline realistic characters? How did their romance build believably? How did the suspense build?

3. What about the setting was clear and appealing?

4. As a bodyguard, Don felt that he had certain rules to follow so he wouldn't fail or disappoint/hurt others. Are there rules in your life that you live by? What rules does God's word provide for us? In what ways are these rules similar or different from the ones you have developed?

5. Caroline felt betrayed by her deceased fiancé. She held on to her anger instead of forgiving him. What does God's word say about forgiveness? What did forgiving him do for Caroline? Can you tell of a time when you had to forgive someone? How did forgiving impact your life?

6. Don was afraid he'd end up hurting those he loved just as his father had done. Are the behaviors of our parents handed down to us? If so, how do we not repeat their mistakes? If not, can you discuss why?

7. Discuss how the lies we tell ourselves can prevent us from our faith and from loving others. Where do these lies come from?

8. Though Don had faith and knew God had intervened in his life on many occasions, he still couldn't understand why God answered some prayers and not others. Caroline said the answer is sometimes just a no. Discuss how God answers our prayers. Can you tell of a time when you did receive an answer? Was it the one you'd hoped for?

9. Though Caroline knew her adoptive parents loved her, she still longed to know the story of her biological parents. How can knowing someone else's story help us or hinder us?

10. The people in the Maddox family had a complicated and dysfunctional relationship. What are your family dynamics? Discuss how the relationships in a family strengthen or weaken us as individuals.

11. Elijah blamed himself for not protecting his daughter. Though he had no culpability in Isabella's murder, he felt that had he not let her go off to college, she'd be alive. In what way is this misguided? How can we protect those we love?

12. Did you notice the scripture in the beginning of the book? What do you think God means by these words? What application does the scripture have in your life?

13. How did the author's use of language/writing style make this an enjoyable read? Discuss whether you would or would not read more from this author.

14. What will be your most vivid memories of this book? What lessons about life, love and faith did you learn from this story?

INSPIRATIONAL

Wholesome romances that touch the heart and soul.

celebrating 15 YEARS

COMING NEXT MONTH
AVAILABLE FEBRUARY 14, 2012

DANGEROUS IMPOSTOR
Falsely Accused
Virginia Smith

THE ROOKIE'S ASSIGNMENT
Fitzgerald Bay
Valerie Hansen

PROTECTING THE PRINCESS
Reclaiming the Crown
Rachelle McCalla

SHATTERED IDENTITY
Sandra Robbins

REQUEST YOUR FREE BOOKS!

2 FREE RIVETING INSPIRATIONAL NOVELS
PLUS 2 FREE MYSTERY GIFTS

Love Inspired®
SUSPENSE

YES! Please send me 2 FREE Love Inspired® Suspense novels and my 2 FREE mystery gifts (gifts are worth about $10). After receiving them, if I don't wish to receive any more books, I can return the shipping statement marked "cancel". If I don't cancel, I will receive 4 brand-new novels every month and be billed just $4.49 per book in the U.S. or $4.99 per book in Canada. That's a saving of at least 22% off the cover price. It's quite a bargain! Shipping and handling is just 50¢ per book in the U.S. and 75¢ per book in Canada.* I understand that accepting the 2 free books and gifts places me under no obligation to buy anything. I can always return a shipment and cancel at any time. Even if I never buy another book, the two free books and gifts are mine to keep forever.

123/323 IDN FEHR

Name	(PLEASE PRINT)
Address	Apt. #
City	State/Prov.	Zip/Postal Code

Signature (if under 18, a parent or guardian must sign)

Mail to the **Reader Service:**
IN U.S.A.: P.O. Box 1867, Buffalo, NY 14240-1867
IN CANADA: P.O. Box 609, Fort Erie, Ontario L2A 5X3

Not valid for current subscribers to Love Inspired Suspense books.

**Are you a subscriber to Love Inspired Suspense
and want to receive the larger-print edition?
Call 1-800-873-8635 or visit www.ReaderService.com.**

* Terms and prices subject to change without notice. Prices do not include applicable taxes. Sales tax applicable in N.Y. Canadian residents will be charged applicable taxes. Offer not valid in Quebec. This offer is limited to one order per household. All orders subject to credit approval. Credit or debit balances in a customer's account(s) may be offset by any other outstanding balance owed by or to the customer. Please allow 4 to 6 weeks for delivery. Offer available while quantities last.

Your Privacy—The Reader Service is committed to protecting your privacy. Our Privacy Policy is available online at www.ReaderService.com or upon request from the Reader Service.

We make a portion of our mailing list available to reputable third parties that offer products we believe may interest you. If you prefer that we not exchange your name with third parties, or if you wish to clarify or modify your communication preferences, please visit us at www.ReaderService.com/consumerchoice or write to us at Reader Service Preference Service, P.O. Box 9062, Buffalo, NY 14269. Include your complete name and address.

Louisa Morgan loves being around children.
So when she has the opportunity to tutor bedridden Ellie,
she's determined to bring joy back into the motherless
girl's world. Can she also help Ellie's father open his
heart again? Read on for a sneak peek of

THE COWBOY FATHER

by Linda Ford,
available February 2012 from Love Inspired Historical.

Why had Louisa thought she could do this job? A bubble of self-pity whispered she was totally useless, but Louisa ignored it. She wasn't useless. She could help Ellie if the child allowed it.

Emmet walked her out, waiting until they were out of earshot to speak. "I sense you and Ellie are not getting along."

"Ellie has lost her freedom. On top of that, everything is new. Familiar things are gone. Her only defense is to exert what little independence she has left. I believe she will soon tire of it and find there are more enjoyable ways to pass the time."

He looked doubtful. Louisa feared he would tell her not to return. But after several seconds' consideration, he sighed heavily. "You're right about one thing. She's lost everything. She can hardly be blamed for feeling out of sorts."

"She hasn't lost everything, though." Her words were quiet, coming from a place full of certainty that Emmet was more than enough for this child. "She has you."

"She'll always have me. As long as I live." He clenched his fists. "And I fully intend to raise her in such a way that even if something happened to me, she would never feel like I was gone. I'd be in her thoughts and in her actions every day."

Peace filled Louisa. "Exactly what my father did."

Their gazes connected, forged a single thought about fathers and daughters...how each needed the other. How sweet the relationship was.

Louisa tipped her head away first. "I'll see you tomorrow."

Emmet nodded. "Until tomorrow then."

She climbed behind the wheel of their automobile and turned toward home. She admired Emmet's devotion to his child. It reminded her of the love her own father had lavished on Louisa and her sisters. Louisa smiled as fond memories of her father filled her thoughts. Ellie was a fortunate child to know such love.

Louisa understands what both father and daughter are going through. Will her compassion help them heal—and form a new family? Find out in
THE COWBOY FATHER
by Linda Ford, available February 14, 2012.

Love Inspired Books celebrates 15 years of inspirational romance in 2012! February puts the spotlight on Love Inspired Historical, with each book celebrating family and the special place it has in our hearts. Be sure to pick up all four Love Inspired Historical stories, available February 14, wherever books are sold.

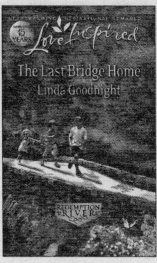